Julia Holland has worked as an advertising copywriter, and editor of an environmental newsletter for business, and has written English language text books for Taiwanese students.

Her first children's novel, "Through the Doorway", was published in 1997, followed in 1998 by a young adult novel, "Nothing to Remember".

Julia was born in England in 1954, moved to Australia in 1990, and now lives with her teenage daughter in Queensland.

Her interests include world religions and myths, travel and the environment.

Also by the author

Storybridge series
Through the Doorway

Young Adult Fiction
Nothing to Remember

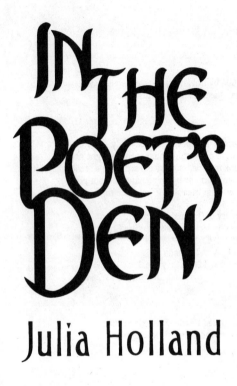

In the Poet's Den

Julia Holland

University of Queensland Press

First published 2000 by University of Queensland Press
Box 6042, St Lucia, Queensland 4067 Australia

Typeset by University of Queensland Press
Printed in Australia by McPherson's Printing Group

Distributed in the USA and Canada by
International Specialized Book Services, Inc.,
5804 N.E. Hassalo Street, Portland, Oregon 97213–3640

Sponsored by the Queensland Office
of Arts and Cultural Development.

Cataloguing in Publication Data
National Library of Australia

Holland, Julia, 1954– .
  In the poet's den.

  I. Title. (Series : UQP young adult fiction).

A823.3

ISBN 0 7022 3149 5

For friends who have shared
the way.

From the words of the poet men take what
meanings please them;
Yet their last meaning points to thee.
Rabindranath Tagore 1861–1941

To Sarita
With love.

dalia.

December 2000

ONE

Summer heat poured through the flyscreens the day Daniel disappeared. Even the late afternoon storm clouds that smothered the sun did nothing to diminish it or to deaden the sound of cicadas drilling the heavy air like demented dentists.

"Quick! Hannah!" The urgent yell from the kitchen made me drop my homework and run.

Mum was watching the early news as she often does while she prepares dinner. She simply pointed at the screen and the newsreader said the rest in her usual tone of exaggerated earnestness.

"*... reports say the shooting occurred about ten pm last night in the remote hinterland property used by members of the cult 'The New Tribe'. The police were tipped off by an anonymous phone call but by the time they arrived at the scene the leader of the cult, known simply as 'The Poet', and his followers had disappeared. Locals estimate that as many as forty people may have been living on the hundred hectare-property that was once the home of eccentric aviator Mal Mulholland. The 22-year-old victim of the shooting was flown by helicopter to the Gold Coast hospital where she is in a serious condition in a coma. The distraught parents of the girl said they had no idea their daughter*" was involved with the cult but thought she was living with friends at Mermaid Beach. Police are keen to interview any cult members or anyone who has information on the identity or whereabouts of the so-called 'Poet' ... In other news today, the Premier defended the government's decision to allow a 900-room resort and six-storey shopping complex on environmentally sensitive coastal wetlands ..."

My first reaction was horror as I imagined Daniel the possible victim. Relief followed when it became clear that the victim was female. Then, within seconds, there was the nagging doubt that would stay with me for months to come. Could Daniel have been the one who shot her?

Neither Mum nor I said anything. Silence encased us even though sounds still stirred the clammy air. Sounds of cicadas drilling. Sounds of a newsreader: ... *the shopping complex will be the largest in Queensland and will create an entirely new shopping experience, the Premier promised* ...

The day Daniel disappeared was not the beginning of our troubles, and it was a long way from being the end of them, but for us, his family, it was a turning point.

TWO

My first memory of Daniel is also my first memory of myself. Daniel was about four or five. I would have been three.

We are sitting at opposite sides of the wooden kitchen table. Ross is beside Daniel and Mum and Dad are at either end. We're at the old house where the last dregs of daylight used to spill through the kitchen window and collect in oblong pools amongst the dinner dishes.

Daniel is thumping the table with determined fists and shouting "More! More! More! More! More!" I like to think it was chocolate pudding that evening but it may have been some other favourite.

No other words come with the memory but Dad looks angry and Mum looks what? Apologetic? Scared? Powerless? Exasperated? They glance at me and I am aware that I am okay. It is Daniel who is making things bad. *I* am good. *I* will not do what Daniel does. Perhaps I wanted more pudding too, but Mum gives me a half-smile which says "*You're* a good girl Hannah" and that tastes sweet enough.

"More! More! More! More! More!" Daniel's shouting and thumping get more insistent, despite Dad rising like a giant from his chair. Daniel is carried to his room, kicking, screaming.

When Dad returns to the table we all sit in careful silence. We can still hear Daniel's shouting, muffled only by the panelled wall, "More! More! More! More! More!"

A fly loops lazily across the table and lands on Daniel's dish.

Daniel has always been part of my life; a familiar bit of living furniture like Mum and Dad and Ross. Ross is six years older than me and seemed to exist in the background with the adults, but Daniel and I were like two climbing plants growing up the fence together. Because he had a headstart, I always looked up to him, took shelter in his shadow when storms or scorching sun brought outside challenges to our usually predictable garden.

These days Daniel himself is a storm. Not a full-on, raging storm but a threatening mass of dark clouds advancing over the mountains, with occasional forks of lightning hinting at its destructive force.

Between the chocolate pudding and the storm are hundreds of other images of Daniel which I now shuffle and rearrange, trying to make sense of the events which turned him from my closest childhood companion to someone I no longer know or understand, someone who could walk out on us and tell us we are no longer his family. He says the New Tribe is his family now.

The last time we saw him was back in winter when he left with just a few bags and boxes, bundled into the back of a friend's ute. The sulphur-crested cockatoos were squawking like angry seagulls and circling the old pine in the neighbours' garden. Their jagged voices echoed the discord in our lives but everything else was mockingly bright. The first poinsettias of winter were scarlet stars above the garden fence and the sky was a vivid blue that almost hurt your eyes. It was as if only *we* in all creation failed to shine that day, as if only *we* had lost the colour from our lives.

Mum was red-eyed and slow as she made coffee no one wanted. Dad had gone out, still tense after the final argument with Daniel the previous evening. I hung around on the sidelines, not knowing what to do or say.

When the last bag was heaved over the side of the ute, I ran and grabbed Daniel's arm, though I knew he was beyond reach already. "You don't have to go. Don't leave with these bad feelings. Don't we count for anything?"

"Let go!" he said throwing off my hand. "Don't any of you understand? I'm going to my new family."

"Let the man go," said his friend, Troy, with just a hint of kindness. "He's not going to the ends of the earth, you know."

But it seemed like he was.

For a while I blamed Dad as much as I blamed Daniel. To understand that, you have to know Dad. The argument the previous evening was typical. Dad never manages to defuse a situation. If it's potentially explosive, he throws petrol on it.

Daniel was complaining about his part-time job at the wholesale palm nursery.

"I can't go on doing this much longer. It's not work experience, it's slave labour!"

"I warned you this is how it would turn out if you blew school," Dad said, as he'd said so many times before.

"Get off me! One mistake and that's it: Daniel is now a disaster!"

Daniel got thrown out of school for what the principal called "a drug offence". It was a symptom of Daniel's troubles not the cause of them.

"Do a TAFE course. Study. Get into computers."

"I hate computers. I want to do something that matters; not some crappy job in an office."

That made Dad worse. He has his own computer business, advising companies and writing programs. He could give Daniel a job if Daniel was interested.

"What are you going to do that matters? Discover a cure

for cancer? Save homeless dogs? Feed the starving millions? Eradicate cane toads?" Dad helped himself to more salad.

"I just don't see the point in working to live, living to work. I want to make a difference."

"Daniel, I've been there, done that. We *invented* idealism in the sixties. In Vietnam, I saw things I hope you'll never see. When I got back I marched in peace demos. But it all boils down to money. Peace protesters didn't stop the war. Money stopped the war. It was costing the American government too much and they realised they could never win."

One of the annoying things about Dad is that you can never do or say or think anything that *he* hasn't done or said or thought before. What's more, he *now* knows better and wouldn't do or say or think anything so pointless.

"The Poet says we can each take responsibility in our own lives ..."

That's when Dad went ballistic. "I don't want to hear about this crazy guru. All those types are in it for the money. Or they're power crazy."

"You're the one who's power crazy! No one can do anything in this house unless it gets your personal stamp of approval. What gives you the right to criticise me? If this is life, I don't think much of it so far. And I'm not going to shovel shit among the palm trees for peanuts so some greedy bastard can get rich. I may be messing up but I won't end up like you!" He strode towards the front door.

"Daniel!" Dad bellowed.

Daniel slammed the door on his way out.

THREE

After Daniel left, we felt like less of a family. Ross had settled into uni in the UK, too far away for frequent visits, and now I was the lone child left at home. But it wasn't just being the only child that made the family seem thinner and less connected. Unspoken words like icy splinters hung between Mum and Dad above the dining table every evening. I was glad when Dad was working late and just Mum and I sat down to dinner.

So was Mum. But she made excuses for him.

"Your Dad wasn't always like this," she said when a few days had rubbed the sharpest edges off our shock at Daniel leaving. "When I met him in Vietnam, he was ..."

"... a brave and handsome soldier who swept you off your feet!"

"You could put it that way! But he could be critical even then. He'd had enough of the war and was lecturing everyone about how stupid the government was for sending young Aussies to fight in a war no one believed in."

"So why did he go to start with?"

"He was conscripted in the ballot. He could have been a conscientious objector and served his time here, but his adventurous spirit won through. When he got home, he joined the peace rallies. He's always spoken out for what he believed in. He liked the fact that *I* was doing something I believed in. I'd *chosen* to go and help, whereas he had ended up in Vietnam through circumstances.

"How could you choose to go somewhere like that? There must have been easier ways to make a living."

"I'd arrived in Australia after travelling overland from England — I'm sure I've told you all this before — and Australia seemed so sterile and suburban after Asia. When the nursing recruitment agency suggested Vietnam, I knew that was somewhere I could make a difference."

"Wasn't it awful?"

"It was terrible. There were never enough medical supplies, the streets smelt of open sewers, the dust got into everything. When it wasn't dusty, it was raining for weeks. Everything went mouldy. Training in London hadn't prepared me for dealing with third-world conditions." Mum's face brightens when she talks about Vietnam despite the bad things she experienced there. I suppose it's some sort of passion.

"Rather you than me."

"It's something you could only understand if you'd been there. I don't think I could have married someone who hadn't been there too. Sharing that made us closer and we felt sort of special, as if we'd *lived* in a way other people hadn't."

"Was Dad like Daniel?"

"In what way? He was pretty tough then. In some ways Daniel is more like me. But it's different now."

"Sure it's different, Mum. We even have electricity!" My patience with these heart-to-heart conversations was limited.

"No, everything is different," she continued, ignoring my comment. "We felt we could make a difference then. It was an optimistic time. We were all going to be richer, more loving, more free, more exciting than our parents. We could drop out of jobs and drop into another one. We could do anything, be anything."

"And we can't?"

"It's tougher for you."

The first few weeks after Daniel's departure I felt lethargic. Schoolwork seemed to take as much effort as digging a shovel full of clay. Even Sam, who had filled my thoughts for months, and occasionally smiled in my direction, seemed less important. There were too many other girls after him anyway and he probably smiled at all of them in just the same way. Sometimes I get tired of trying to compete with people who were born looking gorgeous. Everyone *says* appearance shouldn't matter but everyone *acts* like it does.

It's not that I'm awful looking or anything, but sometimes I think that if I were super-model stunning, Sam would definitely ask me out and my life would be wonderful. Daniel was always looking for something to make his life better too. First there was a new Game System. In his first year of high school he nagged Dad endlessly, even did chores for extra money. Then it was the latest games to go in it.

Next there were the Nike shoes. He would never be anyone to be reckoned with unless his footwear set the tone. We all know you can't wear just *any* clothes if you want credibility, but for Daniel those boots were the Holy Grail.

Before long it was an electric guitar that was his path to fame, fortune and lasting happiness. Mum drew some money out of her savings and gave him one for a birthday present.

Then in Year 10 he went really weird. Suddenly no one and nothing was right for him any more. He shut himself in his room with full-blast heavy metal music. Even though his room is at the far end of the house, neither Mum nor Dad could tolerate it for more than an hour at a time. When he played his guitar, which wasn't often, it sounded like an anguished animal.

It was around the "anguished animal" time that Mum and

Dad started arguing about how to deal with Daniel. Mum's argument was always that Dad should be more understanding; Dad said that Mum had spoiled him and he had to be *forced* to toe the line. It was never quite clear how he could be *forced*. There came a time when he refused to comply with their attempts to discipline him. If he was grounded, he would wait till Dad was out and then just leave. Mum would say, "You know you can't go out, Daniel," but he would ignore her. When Dad came home he would shout at Mum for letting Daniel go. Occasionally Daniel came home drunk.

Then there was the scrape with the police that shocked some sense into him for a month or two. He was with some older guys and they piled a stolen car into someone's garden wall. The car actually belonged to one of the guy's cousins and Daniel said he thought they had permission to use it. That, and the fact he was only fifteen at the time, got him off with a warning but not before he'd been questioned and fingerprinted. It was a major drama, of course, with Dad having to go down to the police station and bring him home.

While all this was going on, I wasn't exactly a goody-two-shoes, but no one was likely to notice me bending the rules while Daniel was snapping them to bits and throwing the pieces over his shoulder.

The drugs incident wasn't exactly a surprise to me — I knew who he was hanging around with — but Mum and Dad were shocked. The idiots were caught smoking it in the bush beyond the school one lunchtime.

Expulsion from school was automatic and it jolted Daniel. The first thing I wanted to say to him was "How could you have been so stupid?" but I swallowed it back. Dad went wild. Mum looked hurt for weeks. Once when both of them were out and Daniel was sitting in the yard watching a fig bird on a banana plume, I tried to talk to him about it.

"What are you going to do now?" I asked.

"I don't know." I think he was close to tears but his dark

side-curtain of hair hid his face. "The whole thing is shit, Hannah. They make me feel like a criminal."

"Why did you do it?"

"Why not? You know what it's like. You have to try things, don't you? I don't know. It didn't seem such a big deal until we got caught."

"I mean why *there*? Someone was bound to see you sneaking off there?"

"I don't know. It was stupid. Sometimes you can't really imagine that the worst will happen until it does. And Dad's a hypocrite. Mum told me he smoked dope when they were young."

"What are you going to do now? Mum's talking about State High."

"No way. I can't stand being treated like a kid any more."

"But what will you do without finishing Year 12?"

"Be a rock star? Or an artist or a poet? Be famous, be rich — isn't that the goal?"

"You could be."

"Get real."

"You're great with music — and lyrics. You're better than average at school work."

"Better than average isn't good enough. Anyway, I won't be going to uni now. Black Sheep Daniel won't be following in Ross's footsteps and making everyone proud."

"Surely there's something you'd like to do?"

"If there is, I haven't got a chance of doing it. Even if I could still get to uni, I'm not sure I'd want to waste another chunk of my life learning stuff I'm not interested in so I can compete with other people who've also learnt stuff they're not interested in just so they can compete with me. And what's the guarantee I'd get a job then?"

"But *someone's* got to get the jobs. It could be you."

"It's irrelevant now anyway. If I'm *really* lucky I might be able to fill shelves at the supermarket and earn enough to pay the rent in some crappy hovel." He ripped the seed head off a blade of grass.

I didn't know what else to say. I could see how he was seeing things. You can't help envying those people who are born super-athletic or ultra-beautiful or totally skilled at something. I suppose I'm more of an optimist than Daniel though and mostly I believe I'll get a reasonable life together somehow.

"Don't you ever wonder what the point of life is?" Daniel sighed. "I mean, there must be more to it than working your guts out for the 4-wheel drive in the garage and, if you're lucky, enough money to have a few weeks holiday away from the boring life you lead the rest of the time." He chucked a pebble into the purple bougainvillea and walked back inside without waiting for an answer.

Half of me wanted to run after him and say something to make him feel better, the other half wanted to yell "Get over it, Daniel!" But I didn't do either.

FOUR

Neither Mum nor Dad seemed to know how to deal with Daniel's expulsion from school. Dad gave a predictable speech about being very disappointed, that this was the sort of thing he'd been warning Daniel would happen if he didn't wake up to himself, and that Daniel had better get out and find himself some work immediately. Mum hovered around anxiously like a bee that can't find a flower, trying to smooth things over for Daniel without going against Dad, trying to calm Dad's anger without alienating Daniel. Daniel spent more time in his room and I tried to ignore the whole thing, daydreaming about Sam and trying to keep up with homework assignments. If anything, I worked harder, as if I could somehow make up for Daniel's sin.

For a while I felt embarrassed at school. I imagined people pointing me out — "*She's* the one with the brother who was expelled". Even those who lived pretty close to the edge themselves weren't exactly sympathetic. I felt the teachers were watching me too, watching for any signs that I might be going down the same track as my brother. For the first time, I wished Daniel *wasn't* my brother; I would happily have swapped him for a brother who didn't create fallout in my life. We'd come a long way since my first day at high school when Daniel had introduced me to his mates, finishing with a casual "She's cool". Then, I'd puffed up with all the importance of a Year 8 who's been rescued from the shaky bottom rung of the school ladder, and I wouldn't have swapped him for anything.

FIVE

It was Melissa who first got Daniel interested in the New Tribe.

He'd met her at an intro evening for a multi-level marketing company called Mega-Nutrition. They'd both answered an ad which said there were job opportunities for creative people with initiative. When he realised what it was all about, Daniel left at half-time and met Melissa sneaking away too. They'd laughed and said it was more like a religion than a job, which is kind of ironic considering she started inviting him to meditation evenings. I hadn't realised that's where he was going until a few weeks later.

I asked Daniel if he was going to hear "Matted Monkeys", a local band he likes.

"No, I'm going to Melissa's ..."

"Melissa? The Mega-Nutrition girl?"

"Come if you want. She has heaps of friends. You can always leave before the meditation."

"You've been meditating?"

"A couple of times."

I'd already told my friend Tori that I'd go to Matted Monkeys, and Sam was likely to be there, so I wasn't about to change plans.

▲ 15

I guess it was a couple of months later that I first heard of "The Poet".

Daniel had started work at the palm nursery and was suffering from working in the summer heat. He came home tired, sweaty and dirty every day. On Friday he announced that he was going away for a long weekend, a "creative retreat" in the Border Ranges.

"That sounds like a nice break," said Mum. "Is it a TAFE thing?"

"Just a group of friends who get together to explore their ideas."

"Is it expensive?"

"No — free in return for a few hours work helping to fix the place up."

"How will you get there?" Mum's inclined to treat us both as if we're still kids. She'd probably tell him to remember his clean jocks next!

"With friends of Melissa."

I could see that Mum was curious, but she had stopped questioning Daniel over the last year or so. Now that he was legally almost an adult, she took the view that she couldn't really stop him doing what he wanted.

"What's this retreat all about?" I asked him later when he was slumped in front of the TV.

"Poetry, music, that kind of thing. It's run by a guy they call 'The Poet'." He didn't take his eyes off the TV where a slender, tennis-teen with long blonde hair was autographing people's programs. She hadn't even won her match, but the crowd was more interested in her than in the plainer-looking winner.

"Are you and Melissa going out?"

"No … It's not about that. They're people I can be myself with."

"And you can't be yourself with us? Aren't we 'creative' enough for you?"

"Don't bug me, Hannah, I'm trying to watch this."

The tennis-teen flicked her long blonde ponytail over her shoulder and waved to the crowd, before leaving the court.

After that, Daniel often went away for the weekend. He was still distant from us but he was happier.

A couple of months into this phase, he tried to persuade me to go along with him one weekend.

"You might really like it. And The Poet is amazing. Things actually make some kind of sense when you hear him talk."

"Meaning-of-life stuff?"

"You could call it that — if you wanted to be simplistic. He covers heaps of ground, Hannah. It's not the sort of thing you can sum up in a few sentences."

"Give me some clues then."

"Well, for a start he says we've lost touch with the most real part of ourselves … Don't ask if you're going to give me that expression when I tell you."

"Sorry. Carry on."

"He's formed this group — The New Tribe — to get us back to thinking cooperatively and he's developing special rituals to mark important passages in our lives. The theory is that we make life painful for ourselves when we're obsessed with our self-centred little worlds. We've lost touch with our sense of being part of the Whole. We don't mature properly in western society."

"So you really think he's got some sort of answers no one else has discovered?"

"It probably sounds crazy to you, but after I listened to him last Sunday, it seemed as if all the colours were brighter, as if someone had switched a light on."

"Yes, it sounds crazy! What's his real name, anyway? Why 'The Poet'?"

"I don't know his real name. Everyone calls him 'The Poet' because he speaks about living life as a poem, taking time to see the beauty, finding space for what's between the words."

He suddenly had that same sparkiness that Mum gets when she talks about Vietnam and her travels in Asia.

Why couldn't he generate this enthusiasm for something normal?

"I don't think it's my sort of thing, Daniel. Anyway, I've got *heaps* of work to do on my history assignment and I need to take some streetscapes for photography club."

I've sometimes wondered what would have happened if I had gone that weekend. Now I think I should have found out more about it so I could have understood what made him leave us. I had strange images of robed monks meditating and everyone shuffling around in a trance, but I probably picked that up from TV. And if I had gone, would they have brain-washed me too?

Although I was sceptical about Daniel's new enthusiasm, I didn't take it too seriously. It was only later when people used the word "cult" about the New Tribe that I started to see it as something much more sinister. And of course when Daniel walked out on us, I suddenly understood just how much he had changed and what a hypnotic influence The Poet was having on him.

Sometimes I think it was the name "The Poet" that appealed to him. He often used to write poetry himself and maybe that gave him special status in the group. He wrote this one not long before he got involved with The New Tribe.

He shuts the front door too loud,
Becomes part of the work-bound crowd,
Makes for familiar city towers
To sacrifice his daylight hours
A slave to his next inflated bill
Has to keep running just to stand still.
Caught in the wheels of dull routine,
A tiny cog in the money machine,

He assumes his well-perfected style,
Affixes his worn-out pin-on smile,

Hides his doubts with too bright faces,
Protects his mind from open spaces,
Drinks after work in a noisy bar,
Drives away in his flash-trash car,
Goes home each night to his show-piece nest
Detached and cool, like all the rest.

Saturday he shines the status symbol collection,
Has friends around for drinks and inspection,
Takes the stage with his tick-tock wife,
Seeking applause for their One Act life.
Their friends are the carefully chosen kind,
They may look bright but they're just as blind,
Their voices too loud, their praises too high,
They always go home when the beer runs dry.

Now they're alone the pretence is weak,
They talk to each other but their eyes don't speak,
They're held together by the way they live,
No more to lose, no more to give,
Avoid any thoughts of their future or past,
Scared it'll end, scared it'll last.
So they'll live forever in bright-facade town,
Afraid to stand up in case they fall down.

I hoped that wasn't the way he viewed our family, the way he saw Mum and Dad.

SIX

Although Mum sometimes talked to me about Daniel after he left, there seemed to be an unspoken rule that we didn't mention him when Dad was around. I had a horrible feeling that we'd let him go too easily and now we were just pretending nothing unusual had happened. Like a stone thrown into a pond, once the ripples had subsided Daniel ceased to exist.

I thought about ways I could get out beyond Mount Barney to visit him and persuade him to come home. Then I'd criticise myself for making too much fuss and I'd focus on schoolwork, Sam, and maybe buy a new CD to cheer myself up. Sometimes I'd eat too much and then start worrying that I was getting fat. If I put on weight my chance of ever going out with Sam would be gone forever.

I hate to admit it, but school wasn't so satisfying now there was no Daniel to compete with. I hadn't realised how much I'd lived off comparison until there was no one in the family to compare myself with. If I got an "A", it was just an "A". There was no hidden pleasure of having worked harder or being "better" than Daniel. Mum and Dad and the teachers were used to me being sensible and hard-working so they didn't even bother to encourage me any more. Sometimes I wanted to wriggle away from the expectations and the pressure, but it wasn't really an option.

We hardly told anyone where Daniel was. Mostly we were vague and said he'd moved out and was living with friends. It seemed like a black mark that he'd turned his back on us and joined a strange group of people at a commune in the country. Mum told Ross when he made his monthly phone call. Maybe she told a friend or two. I doubt Dad told anyone. I told my friend Tori.

"Weird," she said. "How did he get into something like *that*?"

When I saw her disdainful look, I shrugged. "These things happen. It'll sort itself out." I was less confident than I sounded, but suddenly I didn't want to tell her anything else about it. She comes from a picture-book home where even the cat has an engraved medallion with its name and telephone number in case it goes missing. I love her bold and bright approach to everything, but she always seems shocked at the unpredictable crumples in other people's lives. She's sympathetic, sure, but in a way that makes you feel like you're not quite normal.

When the news of the shooting came on TV, it blew apart our silence as surely as if the bullet had been aimed at us.

"Someone's been shot at Daniel's commune!" Mum said to Dad the minute he came in the door.

Dad's face sagged and lost colour for a moment as the shock hit. "Daniel?"

"A girl is in hospital. They didn't say who shot her."

Dad sat at the table and considered it all for a minute. "Daniel wouldn't have done it," he said. "He's too much of a bleeding heart."

"I don't know …" said Mum.

"No way, Nicole. I couldn't even get him to go fishing because he was sorry for the fish!" Dad said it as if he'd pronounced Daniel something from another species.

"That was years ago ..." Mum reasoned.

"What are we going to *do*?" I asked, impatient.

"We'd better call the police," Mum suggested.

"What for?" asked Dad.

"To tell them we have a son with The New Tribe."

"And what will that solve?" asked Dad sarcastically.

I just wanted them to stop arguing and do something. "I think Mum's right. The police don't seem to know much about the place. They were asking for information on the news."

"What do we know?" said Dad. "He'll probably turn up back here tomorrow, frightened by the big bang."

"I'm calling anyway," said Mum, unusually decisive for her.

The police took our details, asked Mum some questions but couldn't tell us much more than we'd heard already.

"They haven't found the gun and everyone who was there is currently a suspect," Mum reported to us. "All but a couple of the cult members have disappeared and they want to interview Daniel if we know where he is. They don't know whether they have all gone their separate ways or whether it is a hostage situation."

"How could one person take them all hostage?" I asked.

"It might not have been one person," said Mum. "There might have been a split in the group or perhaps this 'Poet' has ordered them all into hiding somewhere."

Dad shook his head and covered his face for a moment. "Let's not talk about that man!" he snarled. "God, it's hot in here. I need some fresh air." The screen door wheezed closed and settled with a thunk.

"What now?" I asked Mum.

"Perhaps Daniel will come home," she said with wafer-thin hope.

"And perhaps not!" I said. "We've got to do *something*."

"I don't think there's anything we can do at the moment," she said. "This might all be a storm in a teacup."

"And it might be a bloody Category 5 cyclone!" I said, disgusted with both of them.

I went to my room and sprawled across the bed, staring through the flyscreen at the familiar tree fern. I tried to convince myself that Mum was right, that Daniel might be back here in the morning, happy to have escaped from a situation turned sour. But somehow I knew he wouldn't and this time we couldn't ignore it. This time he might really need us. Whether he was being held against his will or, I hardly liked to think it, if he was on the run from the police, we were the only people he could turn to. But *what* could we do?

I tracked down Melissa's number. She might have disappeared with the others but it was worth a try.

"Melissa? It's Hannah, Daniel's sister."

"Yes, Hannah ..." She shouted at someone to turn the TV down. "I guess you heard the news. Has Daniel called? Is he home?"

"No. I was hoping you'd know where he was. I thought he might have come to your place."

"No. I don't know what's going on. I've got the TV on waiting and hoping for more news. I can't believe it. The Poet is such a peaceful person. It will never feel the same going out there again."

"Have you been there recently? Have you seen Daniel?"

"A few weeks ago. But I expect you've heard from him since then."

"Yes," I lied. "But how was he when you saw him?"

"He was our usual sweet, sensitive Daniel ..."

I hated the way she said "our" and the way she made him syrupy. "Did you see anything suspicious when you were there?"

"Suspicious?" She obviously thought it was a strange choice of word. "No, of course not. It's always so beautiful there — being near the wilderness and the mountains, and being in the presence of The Poet. If I was more surrendered,

I'd have been living there too. I still have an issue with freedom, I think." She gave a slight laugh. "Daniel is *so* mature for his age. He sees his path clearly and nothing gets in his way."

"Will you help me find him?" She was still irritating me but she was my only option.

"I'm sure he'll call soon," she said. "My boyfriend Lennox is there too. He's one of The Poet's right-hand men. He's sure to let me know what's happening. I'll tell him to ask Daniel to phone you."

"Thanks … But Mum spoke to the police and they thought there could be a hostage situation."

"What?"

"The police thought there could have been a split in the group or a mutiny or something."

"The TV didn't say anything about that." She started to sound worried. "I'm sure they've left because the place has been desecrated by the shooting. The police always think the worst of any new spiritual movement. A few lunatics get us all a bad name."

"Would you call me if you hear any news?" I asked.

"Sure. And you call me if the police tell you anything definite."

"You don't think it could have been Daniel, do you? I mean, he couldn't have shot the girl?"

"Daniel? Our dear, sensitive Daniel? I'm surprised you could think such a thing. Of course it wouldn't have been Daniel."

I felt stupid for asking and disloyal because I doubted. "Anyway, I suppose things will be clearer in a day or two."

But they weren't.

SEVEN

Another two miserable days went by. The weather was heavy, heat in every molecule, humid. Mum was moping, martyred, watching TV through every imaginable program, in case of a news bulletin. Dad was disturbed, distracted, with a dangerously short fuse. I was skirting around both of them, trying not to unbalance things further. The first day I still hoped the phone would ring with news, or, better yet, with Daniel himself, but by the second day I was beginning to fear that he had slipped even further away from us. At least we had known where he was before — we *could* have contacted him if we'd tried. Now that he was out of reach, I couldn't believe we hadn't ever visited or written while we had the chance. Sure, he had rejected us, but now he'd think we'd rejected him too.

Wanting to make up for lost time increased my impatience with the situation. Why hadn't the police found him? Why weren't Mum and Dad doing something, *anything*, to pressure the police or to trace Daniel themselves?

By the third day I was depressed. I did drag myself to school, but I seemed to be looking at the world through glasses which made everything look distant and bleak.

"Guess what?" asked Tori on one of the bad days. "Sam was watching you really closely at lunch time."

"What makes you think that?"

"Something to do with the eyes following you. God, cheer up, Hannah. You've been about as much fun as a maths equation recently."

"Thanks. It's always good to have friends."

I'm not sure where I would have gone from there if Melissa hadn't phoned late that afternoon.

Not that it was good news.

"I haven't heard anything from Lennox," she said. "Have you heard from Daniel?"

"No. It's so frustrating just waiting."

"I'm going out to Miralee tomorrow. I don't think anyone will be there but I want to have a look round. I can't understand Lennox not calling. I think I might get more of a feel for what's going on if I can tune in to the energy there. Do you want to come? I've got my sister's car for the weekend and I've cancelled my Saturday violin students."

"Tuning in to the energy" sounded pointless but at least someone was doing *something*, and I wanted to see where Daniel had been living. Perhaps I could take some photos too.

"We'll leave early. Seven. And have breakfast on the way."

Thankfully Mum was doing a night shift at the nursing home and wouldn't be back until after eight, so I just told her I was going out for a picnic with school friends. It was easier not to get into explanations. Dad doesn't take much interest in my social life, and Melissa could have been Tori's sister for all he'd know.

Even that early it was hot. There are days when the heat comes at you directly from the sun and there are days when it comes from everywhere, clinging to you in every droplet of air. That Saturday it came from all directions, creating a damp veil of sweat across every skin surface. Melissa's arms looked cool, pale and delicate holding the steering wheel but her cheeks were flushed pink beneath her fine mist of freckles. We didn't say much while she drove.

We stopped at a little town in the valley between the steep flanks of Tamborine Mountain and the Lamington Plateau. Despite the heat, I could imagine it as a ski resort or perhaps as a location for a cowboy movie. We sat on the wide wooden veranda of a cafe and looked at the large, laminated menus. Melissa took a clip from her bag and piled her wavy auburn hair into a heap on top of her head. It spilled messily in every direction but still made her look elegant and interesting. "I'm starving," she said.

Because she looked so ethereal, I'd imagined she'd have a dainty appetite, but she ordered scrambled eggs, toast, pancakes and an iced chocolate.

"It's not like Lennox," she said once the breakfast choice was settled. "He usually phones at least a couple of times a week."

"How long have you been going out?"

"Three months. I met him at one of the celebration weekends. It was a magnetic thing right from the start. He's so passionate about everything. He's been begging me to move to the commune but I'm not ready for that yet. I do envy people like him and Daniel who *know* what they want."

I thought of Daniel's confusion after school expelled him. He'd never struck me as having the certainty that Melissa obviously saw in him. "What did they do all day there?"

"Didn't Daniel tell you about it? I thought he'd have explained it all — but he's one of those still-waters-run-deep people, isn't he?"

"We haven't spoken to him since he moved to the commune," I admitted. "He never phoned ..."

"I'm surprised. He once told me how close you two were."

"Well, we were," I said, glad to hear it. "But he left after an argument with Dad and it was all a bit messy ..."

"Families can be so claustrophobic for the winged children," she said. "I should know."

"The *winged* children?" I asked, seeing a picture of Daniel with stubby little angel wings.

"The ones that long to fly higher, the ones with the creativity and vision to set their sights beyond the mundane."

"Oh." I suddenly felt decidedly wing*less*, heavy, boring. And was Daniel really a winged one? Okay, he was sensitive, but he was just an ordinary guy who was sometimes lazy, sometimes inconsiderate and hadn't shown any great signs of genius. And his sensitivity, I realised with some resentment, was more that he was sensitive to what impinged on him rather than sensitive to *our* feelings.

"There were a lot of winged children in the commune. The Poet attracts creative people. Daniel was working in the recording studio. Some people did freelance work like architecture or accounting or writing. It was too far for anyone to commute to the city but of course you don't need to with computers."

My picture of the commune adjusted from one of rural simplicity with people toiling over a vegetable plot and milking cows to one with computers and recording studios. "Who was — is — The Poet?"

"We never knew him by any other name. The TV said his name was Moreton."

"How old was he? Where did he come from?"

"About fifty I guess. But ageless. He seemed Australian but he talked a lot about Turkey, India and Tibet — he's lived overseas for large chunks of his life. There's some place in India where he meditated twelve hours a day for forty days, living on water, rice and fruit. Anyway, he encourages us to dispense with labels like nationality which divide us."

"They can unite us," I countered.

"Only in war, or its surrogate — sport," she said. "Do you want anything else to eat?"

Back in the car we lapsed into silence again, Melissa hidden behind sunglasses, me gazing at the scenery.

After a while the country flattened except for the watery blue mountains in the distance. A fine cloud layer did little to cloak the sun; instead it seemed to scatter the brightness everywhere and trap the moist heat. The road was smooth, monotonous, undulating, with only the occasional vehicle rushing past.

It took about an hour before we reached the mountains. Melissa seemed to know her way through the narrow roads bordered by lumpy grassland. Occasionally we passed an old Queenslander in its oasis of protective palms and flowering shrubs, or a shoe-box sized weatherboarded church with storm-worn gravestones.

"Nearly there," said Melissa as we dropped height into a flatter basin beyond the mountains.

I had an urgent desire to turn round and go home. Why had I wanted to see solid proof of this cult? Why was I travelling with this weird person? What if they'd all come back and staged a mass suicide?

We turned into a dirt driveway beneath a tall arch of weather-worn wooden slabs with "Miralee" etched in ancient white. There was also a freshly painted signboard which said "Miralee. Centre for Creativity and Research".

I wanted to ask what the research was, my imagination conjuring up pictures of human guinea-pigs in bizarre laboratories, but my mouth was dry and I took a swig of drink instead. Up ahead was an old stone property partly hidden by trees.

We pulled into a large parking space beyond the trees. Shrubs provided the house with a second line of cover. It would have been a grand country home once — maybe eighty years ago. Now it was looking neglected except at one end where a renaissance was taking place in a cradle of scaffolding. Clean walls, newly painted window frames and fresh supports for the deep roof contrasted sharply with the older portion.

"Isn't it beautiful?" The slamming of Melissa's car-door sounded harsh in the quiet surroundings. Heat formed its own barrier as we walked towards the building. In the shelter of the trees behind us a young magpie ripped the silence, crying hoarsely and insistently until its parent stuffed a grasshopper into its open beak.

"I'll show you the grounds first." Melissa led the way around the side of the house. At the rear, the smooth flagstone path petered out into dry dirt beyond the clipped shrubs and there were half a dozen temporary buildings.

"What were those for?" I asked.

"You don't have to whisper. Mostly extra accommodation. One of them is the recording studio. There's an art room and supplies store too. The pottery and sculpture area is in the old barn over there. The other barn was being converted into an auditorium. I can't believe they would just *leave* after so much work ..." She looked like a forlorn Little Bo Beep.

I followed her to the other side of the house. The flagstone path along a shady walkway led to the even denser shade of a massive frangipani at the centre of a walled garden. Fallen white flowers were nearly as thick on the ground as on the tree itself. A circular wooden bench had been built around the base of the tree, and radial paths led in four directions to archways in the wall. Banks of other plants and shrubs bordered the garden and this cluster of vegetation created a cooler micro-climate.

"My favourite spot," said Melissa. "If you sit here, the mountain is perfectly framed in that archway. Why don't you take a look around the house. I'll stay and meditate for a while. I can still feel the harmony, despite what happened."

"Do you think it would be okay if I took some photos? We've got to do something on the built environment for photography club. It's not the best time of day for light, but

I think I could get something interesting with the scaffolding and stonework."

"I suppose so. You're not thinking of selling them to a newspaper or magazine, are you?"

"Hardly. I can't see anyone wanting a few photos of the house. They'd have sent a professional by now if they did."

I walked toward the house, idly framing dozens of different pictures in the viewfinder but taking only a few. Somehow I wasn't in the mood for it. I put the camera back in my bag and wandered in the deep shade of the portico, stopping to peer in windows. Most of the heavy curtains were drawn but in a few rooms I saw signs of the Tribe's hurried departure. There were clothes on a bedroom floor, dishes on the massive kitchen table and a vase of dead flowers on the mantelpiece in the huge formal lounge room. Where had the shooting taken place? I wondered. Where was Daniel's room? And had he really found what he was looking for here? It made me feel both closer to him and light years apart to imagine his daily walk from the main building down to the recording studio, passing the spot where I was standing.

At the front door I stopped to read the carefully crafted plaque attached to the wall:

The primordial essence that lies hidden,
I, as a poet,
Shall acknowledge it in all humility,
Filling my heart ever
With the perpetual wonder of it.

(Rabindranath Tagore)

I imagined Daniel standing reading those words and, for a nano-second, I thought I understood what had drawn him here. But, before I could catch the feeling, it had slipped through my fingers again.

I flicked at a fly that kept settling on my face and walked on, around the temporary buildings and past the padlocked barns. Had Melissa meditated long enough?

When I walked into the walled garden she opened her eyes. For a moment she looked half angel, half oracle. "I don't think they're coming back," she said.

"Could we look inside the house?" I asked.

Her familiar personality clicked back into place. "I wish I could have shown you round when everyone was here. It was always so vibrant. I don't know if we can find a way in, but let's try."

We walked around again, trying doors, pushing windows, but, if anything had been left open, the police had probably secured it afterwards.

"How about the scaffolding?" I suggested. "Maybe one of the first-floor windows is open."

As we stood there looking up, there was the sound of vehicle tyres on the dirt drive and then doors slammed. Voices. Laughter.

"They're coming back!" I whispered, not sure whether to run and hide or dash out to find Daniel.

"It might not be them," said Melissa warily.

"Who else? The police?" I edged away from our exposed position.

From beyond the shrubbery between us and the car park a tall, ruddy man with a large video camera appeared. Another cameraman, three or four other people and a woman in a vivid pink tight-skirted suit arrived. As soon as the first cameraman saw us, he started running the camera.

We stood like mesmerised animals caught in a car headlight beam.

Another guy with a microphone and some sort of equipment over his shoulder approached us. "Are you members of The New Tribe?" he asked, thrusting the microphone first at me, then at Melissa.

"No." I said.

"Yes, sort of," said Melissa, adjusting her hair.

"Where are the others?" he asked, now concentrating on Melissa and directing the microphone at her.

"I don't know," she said. "Hey, what is all this about?"

"Were you here on the day of the shooting?" the man asked, ignoring her question. The camera was still running behind him.

"No, I wasn't," she said. "Stop. Leave us alone."

"Did you know the girl who was shot?" the interviewer continued.

"I don't want to talk about it," Melissa said. She walked towards the car, dodging the guys who were blocking the path. I followed half a step behind.

"Wait, wait," the guy said, removing his microphone now and hurrying after us. "We're from *Another Day in Queensland*. We're doing a feature on The New Tribe. We want to hear what attracted young people here. What was it all about?"

Melissa still looked dubious.

"Just a few words," he said. "People want to know about this Poet guy."

"Give me a few minutes first," Melissa said.

"They're going to talk in a minute," he said over his shoulder to the following entourage.

Melissa got drinks from the car, wiped the sweat from her forehead and adjusted her hair. "Do I look okay?" she whispered. I nodded. "I'm not sure if I should do this."

"In front of the house would be good," the guy said. He positioned us at the opposite end from the scaffolding. "Yes, you stand with her," he said, manoeuvring me closer to Melissa. "What are your names?"

I'd never been on TV before. I hoped I looked okay and I hoped Melissa would do the talking.

"What attracted you to being a member of The New Tribe?" the guy asked Melissa, giving her an encouraging smile.

"The Poet. I've never met anyone with such an inspiring

vision of how life could be. I believe society needs to rethink its direction and he's saying things that can help everyone."

"And you?" he asked, directing the microphone at me.

"Er, I'm just here to look for my brother …" I muttered.

"Is your brother a member of the Tribe?"

"Yes."

"Are you concerned for his safety?"

"Well, kind of. I mean, we don't know where they are."

"This must be a very traumatic time for you …"

"Er, yes." Then it occurred to me that Daniel might see the program. "We'd really like Daniel to get in touch and let us know he's okay."

"How are your parents taking it?"

"Well, naturally they're worried too."

"I expect the family doesn't feel the same without him …"

"We do miss him."

"Did you have any indication of the violence that was lurking beneath the surface here?" He turned his attention to Melissa again.

"No, it's always been so peaceful, such a welcome retreat from the crazy world," she answered.

"We've heard from locals that this was a commune of free love. Were you involved in relationships here?"

"It was a very loving place," said Melissa. "We all did our best to care for each other."

"Do you think The Poet could be holding people against their will?"

"No, he never wanted anyone here against their will."

"Could there have been a split in the group, one faction against another?"

"It's possible," said Melissa. "But I don't think so."

"Did you know the girl who was shot?"

"Yes, I knew most of the people here."

"Have you visited her in hospital."

"No. I didn't know her very well."

"Do you think this could have been an attempted execution? Someone punished for breaking the rules?"

"Of course not." Melissa started to look exasperated.

"What is the attraction of groups like this?" he continued.

"It's like the plants," Melissa said. "If you have a rare, tender plant, it grows better if it is nurtured with other plants in a garden. It would soon wither and die if it was exposed to the weather on the mountainside."

They didn't use that bit in the TV program. In fact, even though I was suspicious of the cult myself, I was shocked by the misleading patchwork they created.

EIGHT

We watched *Another Day in Queensland* each evening that week. I was dreading seeing myself but keen to hear if they had any other news on The New Tribe. Finally, on the Thursday Mum said they'd been running trailers promising an investigation into the "Bizarre world of a Queensland cult" that evening.

First we had to sit through "How a high fruit diet can improve your sex life". It was pretty tacky really, with couples drooling over each other and making smugly suggestive comments about the benefits they'd enjoyed from eating kilos of strawberries and mangoes.

Finally the segment we had been waiting for.

Earlier this month a shooting at a remote property near the Queensland border drew the country's attention to a bizarre cult called The New Tribe. In a mysterious twist, about thirty young people disappeared before the police could interview them. Dozens of families have been devastated by the disappearance of their loved ones and there are grave concerns for the safety of those who are involved. It is still unclear what triggered the shooting but our reporters uncovered a disturbing picture of the "tribe" which scorns the laws and standards of normal society ... Marina Trott reports ...

The young woman in the vivid pink suit was standing by the "Miralee" sign. *It is here in a remote mansion, nearly a hundred kilometres from the nearest major town, that a guru who called himself "The Poet" created a cult which terrified the local people and destroyed happy families. The full extent of their bizarre practices is only just coming to light. Locals we spoke to suspect that brainwashing, drugs and pagan fertility rites were involved in the cult's rituals.* I glanced at Mum who was watching with horrified attention. *We spoke to Hannah Jarvis, the distraught sister of a cult member, who admitted that her family has been shattered by recent events.* The scene cut to me, looking rather bewildered ... *"We do miss him." "We'd really like Daniel to get in touch and let us know he's okay."* Back to Marina Trott ... *Cult member Melissa admitted that the group indulged in free love orgies but she was loyal to The Poet.* (Cut to Melissa.) *"I've never met anyone with such an inspiring vision." Melissa didn't discount the possibility that warring factions within the organisation were behind the shooting and that other cult members lives may be at risk. The rift within the group was underlined by the fact that she hadn't visited the victim of the shooting in hospital although she knew her well.*

Around the multi-million dollar property, which has been allowed to fall into disrepair, are signs of squalor left by the group that liked to think of themselves as "creative". The camera zoomed in to dirty dishes in the kitchen, an overflowing garbage bin behind a wall, and a broken window on one of the demountable buildings. Next there were a couple of short interviews with local people who thought the people in the cult were "strange", "drugged" or "unfriendly".

The police so far have no leads on the person or persons responsible for the shooting and they are eager to talk to the cult leader who is thought to use the surname Moreton. Moreton does not have a previous criminal record but they are worried that he has a hypnotic influence over his followers and may be mentally unstable. Last weekend, police raided a boat anchored on the New

South Wales Central Coast where they believe Moreton may have been temporarily hiding with some of his tribe, but there was no sign of any cult members.

Meanwhile, families are banding together and have hired a private detective to try to trace the missing people. Scene cuts to a tearful mother. "She has always been so special to us. She was in her first year at uni. She'd worked so hard. She would never have done anything to hurt us before she came under the influence of these people. She phoned the night after the shooting and told us she was okay, but she wouldn't tell us where she was."

Return to Marina Trott ... It's events like these that worry every parent of an impressionable young person. It seems no one is immune from the lure of cults which can strike anywhere, any time. The New Tribe has members from the Gold Coast, Brisbane and northern New South Wales. Most of them were normal, happy young people. Today their parents are left with just memories and the long and painful wait for further news. (Return to the studio presenter.) Something for all parents to think about. And, after the break, the Gold Coast schoolgirls that work part time as prostitutes ...

"It wasn't like that," I said to Mum. "They'd been doing major renovations on the place — and they hardly used any of the things Melissa said."

"But you don't know what went on there," said Mum. "They said drugs and brainwashing and fertility rites."

"I don't think Melissa would be involved in that sort of stuff. She can be annoying but she isn't a junkie. And Daniel wouldn't either."

"I'm going to phone the TV station and get a number for the other parents. I hope the police catch that Moreton and put him behind bars."

Mum had recorded the program and we watched it again later when Dad was home.

"I'm going to call the parents' group," Mum announced when the video finished.

"Don't waste your time," said Dad. "They'll only want money from us for their private detective. Leave the idiots to it, I reckon."

"We've got to do *something*. For all we know, they could be prisoners or about to kill themselves."

"They'll find them just as well without our help. I'm not getting involved with a whinge group. We'll soon hear if there's any news."

Mum said nothing. I found myself increasingly confused. The TV program had stirred up more questions than it had answered and the presenters had deliberately created the worst possible slant on everything. How much could I believe of the danger they implied? I wished Daniel hadn't got us all involved in this situation. I wanted to push it out of my mind and forget him, but I don't seem to have a "delete" button.

I was still rerunning the TV program in my head the next day at school when Sam came up to me.

"Hey, I saw you on TV last night. I didn't know Dan was involved with that weird lot."

"Well …"

"He's just disappeared?"

"Yes." This wasn't the way I wanted a conversation with Sam to go.

"Must be tough for you, eh?"

"Yes."

"Do you want to come to the movies tomorrow?"

"Who's going?"

"I was thinking just you and me?"

"Er. Yes. Okay. Sure. What movie?"

That took my mind off Daniel for the rest of day. At last. Six months of meaningful looks had finally amounted to something.

I was zipping around at home that evening on the jet fuel of anticipation when the phone rang. Please don't let it be Sam calling to cancel the date.

A girl's voice. "Can I speak to Hannah?"

"This is Hannah."

"You don't know me but I saw you on TV last evening. I'm Daniel's girlfriend."

NINE

Her name was Jody and she lived in Brisbane. She wanted to meet me. First she suggested Saturday but I was worried I wouldn't be back in time for the date with Sam so we settled on Sunday and agreed to meet at Roma Street station.

"Do I look okay?" I asked Mum when I'd finally settled on what to wear to meet Sam.

"You look beautiful. But won't you feel a bit over-dressed for the movies?"

Dad looked up from the weekend newspaper. "I think she looks fine. Nice to see you in something smart," he said.

So I went and changed. What was I thinking? What did I usually wear to the movies?

I guess I was smiling like a chat-show host most of the evening. Not that anyone could see in the movies. The movie itself wasn't that great — over-the-top violence and a hopeless revenge story — but my life was looking up at last. After the movie we had coffee and shared a carton of chips. Sam's a born joke-teller and I laughed more than I had for ages. He even paid for a taxi home.

"I had a great time," I said, as the taxi turned into my road.

"Me too. D'you want to watch my cricket match on Tuesday and we could go for a coffee after? Four o'clock on the oval."

"Sure." Trying to keep my enthusiasm under wraps.

No kiss. But I think he thought about it.

The train into Brisbane from the Gold Coast was a refrigerated tube gliding through the countryside. We sped past dams carpeted with mauve, water lilies, secret gardens of grand houses or grotty houses on streets you'd never have any reason to drive down, graffiti on the back walls of shopping centres. And then, after long stretches of anonymous suburbia, the city suddenly appeared in tall, geometric clumps.

Back in the baby-blanket warmth of real air, people quickly disappeared down rabbit-hole stairways. "Meet at the top of the escalators in the food area", Jody had said. She'd be wearing a red T-shirt with *"Life's a bitch And then you die"*.

At first I didn't see her. A sprinkling of people sat at white plastic tables, eating from polystyrene packaging or plain white plates. Then my eyes sifted her from the crowd, a small person with wavy, slightly wild black hair and darkish skin.

Her face looked sad as she stared into her cardboard-cloaked drink, but it transformed with a burst of brightness when I introduced myself.

"I'm so happy to meet you," she said with enthusiasm. "I can see you're Danny's sister. You look more like him in real life than you did on TV." There was a moment's embarrassing pause. "This isn't a great place to talk," she said. "Shall we find another cafe or go to the park or something?"

We headed for a park near the station, with Jody repeating half a dozen times how pleased she was I'd come to talk to her and that she hoped it wasn't a waste of my time.

We found a seat in the dark green shade of a fig tree.

"I really wanted to meet you," I reassured her. "I can't wait for news of Daniel. And I didn't even know he had a girlfriend. How did you meet him?"

"I was living at the commune. When he visited at weekends we always used to talk, but we didn't get together until he came to live with us. We'd still be together now if I hadn't taken a few weeks away to visit Mum. She's was in hospital for an operation and then she was convalescing so I've been looking after my half-brother and sister."

"You're allowed to leave the commune whenever you want to?"

"Of course. The hard part is getting back in! If you're away for more than a couple of weeks, they're likely to give your room to someone else. I was counting on sharing Daniel's space when I went back. Just my luck to have gone away at the wrong moment! I do miss Daniel. I'm going crazy back at home with the kids. I had a letter from Daniel postmarked Port Macquarie but he said not to come. He was expecting to move any day."

"Is he safe? What's happening?"

"I think he's fine."

"It couldn't have been … I mean … Daniel wouldn't have shot that girl, would he?"

"Geez, you're joking! It was probably some local."

"The locals didn't like you?"

"Understatement. We were the greatest threat to Aussie values since the war. There's nothing dissatisfied people like better than an enemy and we were it. You wouldn't believe the stories that went round about us. Every time a sock blew off the clothesline it had obviously been stolen by the "devil children" at Miralee. People wrote letters to the local paper and there were a couple of phone calls threatening to kill The Poet if we didn't leave town."

"Did you take them seriously?"

"Sure we did. Daniel got real protective and said I shouldn't go into town alone. Then a couple of Tribe members were kidnapped by their parents and there was even more reason to move around in groups. One of them was out shopping when she was grabbed. Another guy was told his mother was sick, but when he got home they locked him up and tried to brainwash him into leaving the Tribe."

"Is Daniel ... okay? I mean, when he left home he was kind of depressed. And he's never called us."

"He's the most okay person I've ever met. But we've both had times when nothing makes sense. I used to think it was me, because I've got some Aboriginal blood, because I never knew my Dad. Because my step-dad hated me. Because I didn't do great at school and ended up working in a shitty clothes shop. Don't ever work in a clothes shop. After two weeks I wanted to strangle the customers or rip the stupid stock to ribbons! Have you ever noticed how all the hooks on the hangers face the same way on the rails? When I started fantasising a rebellion of hangers pointing in different directions, I knew I was losing my mind."

"Then you escaped to the commune?"

"The Poet showed me a different way of seeing things. And I realised it wasn't just me. There were people like Daniel who'd had a 'normal' life who couldn't make sense of the world that most people live in either. Sounds corny, I guess, but the Tribe are like the family I've always wanted. People who understand me." She paused for a minute, assessing. "Think of Daniel as being sane and the rest of the world as mad! It's closer to the truth."

"So he was happy there?"

"Of course. The Tribe is such an amazing idea. I used to dream of finding the people my grandma was stolen from. But I don't really belong with them. But I think it's natural for people to live as a group and care for each other. Perhaps it's in my blood even though I'm only a fraction Murri."

"Do you think everyone will go back to Miralee?"

"I don't understand why they left. Daniel's letter was short. He said he was staying at a caravan park, that things had been difficult. And that he was missing me. He said he wanted to see me but we'd have to wait until the fuss died down."

"Is The Poet with them?"

"He was overseas when it happened. The media don't want to know that, of course. They'd rather create a good story than find out the truth."

"Why didn't Daniel come and visit us? While he was living at the commune I mean?"

"He couldn't see any point in going home because none of you understood what he was doing. He said you were great and his mum was okay but he didn't get on with his dad. He thought he'd just spend the whole visit trying to justify his choice, seeing his mum upset, feeling guilty that he'd let you all down somehow. He did laugh that his dad might approve recently when he was put in charge of security!"

"Security?"

"After the phone threats we had to be alert. We couldn't take any chances."

"Did Daniel have a gun for that?"

"If he did, he didn't tell me. It was more a case of checking out the weekend visitors and tradesmen, making sure they were who they said they were. That sort of thing. People don't like anyone challenging the religious rulebook. Look what happened to Jesus!"

"But there have been some really weird cults. You can't blame people for being suspicious."

"I can blame them for not finding out before they judge. I've seen too much of people's prejudice to forgive it easily."

I wanted to ask her how she could be sure The Poet wasn't a megalomaniac manipulating them all, but didn't. I wanted to stay on her side. I wanted to be counted with her and Daniel, not with the ignorant and prejudiced. "If you get to speak to Daniel, please tell him I *really* want to see him."

"That makes two of us."

TEN

The meeting with Jody hadn't exactly reassured me but her news could have been worse.

It seemed there was nothing to do but wait.

In the meantime, things between Mum and Dad hit an all-time low. Monday evening, machete-blade words were hurled through the air. The jagged atmosphere settled through the house, mixing with the humidity. No corner was comfortable. With every breath I seemed to inhale the scouring remnants of combat.

I watched Sam's cricket match only half there. I tried to talk brightly to him afterwards but there was a chasm between me and my words. Perhaps he didn't even notice. He invited me to his place on Saturday to watch the one-day cricket on TV.

I didn't really want to go home. Home seemed claustrophobic. At this time of year, the grass grows jungle-fast, and long arms trail from every shrub hugging the house too tight. I found myself dreading the suffocating walls of vegetation and the threat of violent voices still hanging in the air.

I walked slowly, kicking stones, feeling sorry for myself. This was all Daniel's fault. Or was it Dad's? Or was it The Poet with his hypnotic influence? It just wasn't fair.

When I finally went home, Mum was sitting at the dining table, cradling a mug of coffee, looking as defeated as I felt.

"Something's eating your dad," she said without greeting me or asking about my day at school.

"I heard you arguing."

"He won't talk about it."

"I hope he'll be in a better mood this evening ..."

But he wasn't. I sat staring at my geography book, listening to their ritual verbal punches, wondering whether to go and say something. I was too scared. It's between him and Mum, I told myself. But I wished I could stop them.

The phone ringing was like the bell at the end of a boxing round. I answered it, aware that they would have retreated to their own corners, suspending the fight for a few minutes, the pattern broken by the sudden outside sound. With a little luck it would be enough to stop their slanging match for tonight.

It was Jody.

"Hi Hannah! I spoke to Daniel for a few minutes. He's going to be in Byron Bay on Thursday. Just for the day. Casey is driving up to visit his mother before they go somewhere else they can't tell me about. He asked me to meet him in a cafe there at ten-thirty on Thursday morning."

"Is he okay?"

"He sounded fine as far as I could tell. He was calling from a phone box and he only had a couple of coins so we couldn't talk for long."

"Are you going?"

"Of course I am. D'you want to come?"

"Me?" Stupid question. "Well, I have to go to school ..."

"School? Geez, you're crazy! We'd need to get the bus tomorrow night. There isn't one Thursday that'll get us there in time. We can stay somewhere cheap. A backpackers or camp-site ..."

"Overnight?" My mind seemed to have gone off-duty. I

knew there were plenty of good reasons why I shouldn't do it but I knew that I was going to do it anyway. "Okay. What time's the bus?"

"Five forty-five from Surfers bus station. I'll book the tickets for both of us and you can pick up yours at the check-in desk. I'll be coming through from Brisbane on the same bus. Promise you'll be there!"

A couple of times that evening I reached for the phone to call her back and tell her I couldn't do it, but something stopped me. Mum wouldn't let me take time off school or stay away overnight, so I couldn't tell her what I was going to do. The truth is, I was glad to have an excuse to get away.

ELEVEN

I changed out of my school clothes in the toilets and sat upstairs in a cafe with an hour to spare before the bus was due. The heavy purple clouds had been threatening a storm when I arrived and before long they dropped a dark curtain of rain around the bus station. The smell of cake, coffee, cleaning fluids, plastic and wet hair mingled in the moist air. A couple of backpackers were playing cards in the corner and an older man was doing a crossword at another table. The sound of the coffee machine momentarily eclipsed the sound of tyres swooshing on the wet road outside.

Here was a crossroads of people. Hundreds of stories collided here, stories which may have started thousands of kilometres away or just down the road. By this time tomorrow, new chapters would be opening in new corners of the country. I wondered what new lines would have been written in my life by the time my bus returned me here.

It would be strange to see Daniel after so long. Just the thought of seeing him gave me hope that life could return to normal. Or, if not normal, at least to something less fractured than it had been recently. But would he be pleased to see me? I wished Jody could have warned him I was coming. Was it pure generosity which made her share their limited time with me or did she need me to help cement something with Daniel?

Talking to Mum on the phone against the background bustle of the bus station wasn't easy. Once she got over her initial shock, she seemed more worried about Dad's reaction than anything. I promised to phone and let her know where I was staying when I got there. Of course she made me feel like a traitorous worm, but at least she ended by asking me to give Daniel a hug from her. And she stressed that I *must* tell him he was welcome to come home whenever he wanted.

Replacing the phone, I realised I'd been more worried about the phone call than about the journey. Now I was ready for my bus to arrive. I wondered what time Daniel would leave Port Macquarie. Would he be packing now? And again, would he be pleased to see me?

The giant glistening body of the bus glided into the boarding area. It smelt of warm, wet metal and long, dusty days; of tyres and diesel and dirt from endless roads. Weary-looking travellers got off and retrieved their luggage from its belly.

My seat next to Jody was near the back of the bus. After her initial excitement at seeing me, we didn't talk much until the bus had left the tangled roads and jumbled lights of the shiny, wet Gold Coast and was cruising through the darkening countryside.

"Are you excited about seeing Daniel again?" I asked.

"Excited and terrified!"

"Why terrified?"

"What if he doesn't want to be with me any more? It's different at the commune. It's so easy to flow with the love. Problems lie down and doze in the corners. Out here in the world, they wake up and look for people to eat."

"I guess one of them woke up and went on the rampage the day of the shooting."

"You're still worried Danny might have been involved, aren't you?"

"I don't *think* he's capable of shooting someone. But then I didn't think he'd have stolen a car or got involved with drugs either. I don't feel I know him properly now. He was having trouble when he left and it's not hard to imagine that pain turning ugly."

"I know what you mean. I've got a cousin who copped endless shit from his dad. I mean put-downs every day and beatings whenever his dad had been drinking — which was most nights. When he was nineteen he knifed a bouncer who wouldn't let him into the nightclub. Luckily the bouncer survived, but Jed was in jail for a long time."

"And you didn't see that sort of ... trouble ... in Daniel?"

"Worst I saw was he'd sometimes be distant with me. Guys can be so evasive at times. Then, at other times ... well, that's why I love him! Geez, it's cold in this bus. This isn't air-conditioning, it's refrigeration! Are you going out with anyone?"

"There's a guy at school. Sam. We've just had a couple of dates. I've liked him for ages."

"Funny, I wasn't attracted to Daniel when I first met him. He seemed a bit serious. I thought, what the hell would he want to talk to someone like me for? You can tell you two come from a classy home. My lot are battlers. But he always came and sat with me at meal times. I probably talked too much. I always do. Then one afternoon I was sitting in the garden after The Poet had given a talk. It was like I was just crying for everything that had ever gone wrong in my life. Daniel came and put his arm around me. That's when it really started."

After that, she seemed to settle to her own thoughts while the bus sped onwards.

The rain had stopped by the time we arrived in Byron Bay. The clouds had blown far enough away to reveal the stars and the air was lukewarm, salt and satin mixed.

Jody's enormous bag was the last out of the bus-belly. "You look like you're planning to stay a month!" I laughed.

"I didn't want to tell you before, but I'll leave with Daniel if he wants me with him. They don't need me in Brisbane any more. My home is with The Poet. And with Daniel."

"Selfish like Daniel," I thought. "She doesn't care that I will have to go back alone".

Jody had booked us a cabin at the campsite and while she phoned for a taxi to get us there I phoned Mum. She said Dad was furious with me. And furious with her. I tried not to think about that. I tried not to think about anything.

As we drove through the little town, lights from cafes and restaurants glowed into the night and reflected off every wet surface. A few people sat outside at tables and others were strolling along, window shopping. I'd been feeling hungry on the bus but now I just wanted to get to our cabin and switch off for the day.

At the campsite, the sound of the waves in the bay, the smell of ocean and the feel of sand beneath my shoes recalled long-ago holidays. Dad used to bring a garden shovel with him and he helped build the most impressive sandcastles.

Our cabin was simple, furnished in brown plastic, but quite cosy with its too-dim fluorescent light.

"Food?" asked Jody, as I slumped down on one of the four bunks. "I packed some instant noodles and chocolate. To eat separately of course!"

"Okay." I didn't smile at her feeble humour. "Noodles would be good. I'm tired."

"You're angry with me, aren't you? You're just like Daniel when he's not happy about something."

"I wish you'd told me you were planning to leave with Daniel. I shouldn't have come. I'm going to be in a heap of trouble at home and three's a crowd. I'll feel like little-sister tagging along when Daniel sees me with you."

"He'll be one hundred per cent pleased to see you. I know

it. It'll be a huge surprise for him. I only decided about going with him when I woke up this morning. I'd already booked a return ticket."

I managed a weak smile and a nod which she would probably have recognised as a Mum gesture, if she'd spent any time with the rest of my family.

We both woke early, as revved up as kids on holiday now. "Swim, shower, then breakfast in town," Jody said, rummaging in the enormous bag for her bikini.

The sand was cool and damp underfoot, and the sun had only just risen out of the sea mixing rose through the silver water. The beach was deserted apart from a guy doing tai chi near the headland and a woman jogging towards town.

Plunging into the sweep of gentle surf that caresses the bay, I washed away cobwebs of sticky emotions that had clung to me over the last couple of weeks. Jody powered through the water doing an impressive butterfly stroke and then I took almost a full roll of film while she drew faces in the sand and danced in the surf, gleaming like a manic sculpture, scattering light in showers around her.

The sun had already risen to pale yellow brightness and warmth by the time we were walking into town, our hair still damp.

Cafe owners were putting out chairs and menus, opening their doors for the early risers. Before long the street held a constant movement of people: guys in board shorts; women in muslin; trendy tourists; middle-aged, tame hippie types; people our age with enough ear and body rings to hang a curtain; a girl with beach-blond hair and skimpy shorts wearing heavy boots on tanned legs; a shaven-headed guy spooning food to a tiny baby. Jody seemed to fit right in with her slightly wild hair, a cocoa-coloured lacy top and faded jeans hacked off above the knee. I felt much too squeaky-clean in clothes that were comfortably fashionable at home.

We toured the shops after breakfast and Jody bought a

Japanese kimono and a small wooden box with silver inlay, both for Daniel. I couldn't imagine him wearing the kimono in a hundred years, but she didn't ask my opinion. I wanted to buy him something but didn't have much money. I searched for ages and eventually I chose a key ring attached to a perfect sphere of native wood polished marble-smooth.

Then it was time to find the cafe and wait for Daniel. We sipped nervously at smoothies, our eyes turning to the door every few seconds. When a tall, dark-haired guy in shredded jeans and tatty T-shirt came in, I started wondering if Daniel would have changed a lot. Maybe he would have grown his hair and started wearing purple velvet jackets. Or perhaps he would have cropped his hair to a few millimetres all over and bought a leather vest like the guy serving the drinks.

"Twenty minutes late already! Trust them!" Jody said after turning round to look at the big clock above the counter.

Another thirty minutes went by.

"They could have broken down," Jody said, after looking at the clock for the umpteenth time.

"Are you sure this is the right place?" I asked.

"Positive. He even mentioned the posters on the walls."

We bought another drink.

"They're well over an hour late, now," I pointed out unnecessarily when our orange juice glasses had also been cleared away. "How much longer should we wait?"

"I'll wait all day if I have to. Stay with me until half-past. Then if you get the bags, I won't move from here until you get back."

"Are you sure he meant today?"

"Is either of you Jody?" asked the guy in the leather vest.

"Me," she said.

"There's a phone call for you. It's along the corridor there, just before the toilets. Keep it short. The manager doesn't like customers getting calls here but the guy said it was important."

She kept it short. Less than five minutes. Short, but long

enough for me to imagine car accidents, breakdowns, floods and earthquakes.

Jody came back with less spring in her step and no smile. "They're not coming," she said. "It wasn't Daniel. It was Casey. A farmer found a gun in the bush near the commune yesterday. It had Daniel's fingerprints on it. They heard it on the radio news this morning when they were on their way here. They can't risk being seen so they'll lie low for a few days. Casey said to believe in Daniel. He says it wasn't him, but they'll have to prove it."

"What? I don't understand. If it wasn't him, then why do they have to go into hiding? He could just talk to the police and get it sorted out." I tried to speak quietly but my voice was cracking with the sudden burden of disappointment.

"You have touching faith in the police and our justice system," Jody said, contemptuously emphasising the word "justice".

"Why did he have to get involved with this stupid cult? Why couldn't they just come and talk to us? Or ask us to meet them out of town somewhere?"

"Don't demand answers from me, as if it's *my* fault. I want to see him too, remember."

We were both talking quietly but fiercely, useless words, in a void of shock.

"I shouldn't have come. It's gone from bad to worse," I said. *It's been a complete waste of time and it's your fault for inviting me here*, I thought, plunging into new depths of dejection. "Where were they phoning from?" I asked, as if more information might somehow help.

"About a hundred kilometres south of here, I think. He said they'd left the Pacific Highway and headed inland as soon as they heard the news and it took them a while to find a phone box to call us."

"God, he's stupid! He's stupid if he's innocent and panicked, and he's ultra-stupid if he did it! I don't know why I'm wasting my life worrying about him."

"Give the guy a chance! If his family doesn't support him, who will?" Jody snapped.

"Come on, we'd better get back to the campsite."

I'm not sure if it was too hot to talk or whether we were both lost in our own disappointment as we trudged back in silence. The passers-by who had seemed so colourful and interesting this morning were now an annoyance. I would be happy to get home.

But when I thought about it, home didn't seem so inviting either, with Dad ready to bawl me out, Mum upset, and to top it off, no hope of completing my geography assignment by tomorrow.

My whole life had been hacked into tatters with blunt scissors. If I'd had the means, I'd have been tempted to go into hiding too. I threw Daniel's key-ring, still wrapped in its yellow tissue paper, into the sand dunes beneath the casuarinas.

TWELVE

"Police have a suspect in the mysterious Queensland cult shooting after a gun was found on land near the cult's deserted mansion late yesterday. He is 18-year-old Daniel Jarvis. Daniel is believed to be in hiding with other cult members who have not been seen since the shooting. His parents declined to comment today. The victim, a 22-year-old woman, is still in a coma at the Gold Coast Hospital where her family are keeping a round-the-clock vigil. In other news, American comedienne Paula Hiltberg is to receive a record US$750,000 an episode for another series of her hit comedy, 'Sex-starved and Single' ..."

Mum, Dad and I were now like three unrelated people who only occasionally crossed paths in the course of our domestic lives. Dad ignored me. I didn't even get the expected blast about staying away. Mum avoided Dad and when she spoke to me it was with an expression of someone who has had a nail driven into her forehead. I guess I had now proved myself as unreliable as Daniel and Dad. The police had been to the house to talk to her the previous evening. She hadn't told them Daniel was due to meet me in Byron. She hadn't mentioned Jody or Port Macquarie either.

I tried to shut Daniel out of my mind but my mental gatekeeper was asleep on the job. Occasionally I tried to revive the hope that it hadn't been him, but fingerprints on the gun are hard to ignore. Sometimes I wanted to go and find him, to help him. Other times I told myself that if he was stupid enough to get into this mess, he would have to get himself out of it; it wasn't my problem.

To make matters worse, Sam wasn't really what I expected.

The Saturday date was a flop and I didn't know how to tell him about the problems in my life.

"What's the matter, Hannah?" he asked "You've been pretty quiet all day. Aren't you a cricket fan?"

"It's not that," I said. But somehow I couldn't start to tell him what it was.

After all those months of wondering what it would be like to kiss him, when his lips found mine I pulled away.

"Don't you like me?" he asked, puzzled.

"I did. I do. I just can't cope with this at the moment. It's not your fault."

I didn't let him see me cry. That came later in the evening when I thought about losing him after having wanted him for so long. But it wasn't even losing *him* that hurt. It was losing the comforting cushion of dreams about him.

I wanted to hide from everyone for a while, but the following day Melissa phoned: "Lennox is back. I've been so angry with him for not calling me, but now I understand that they were all so shattered by the shooting. I'm really sorry about Daniel and the gun. I still find it hard to believe myself. I wasn't sure whether to call you, but I thought Lennox might be able to tell you more about what happened. He's happy to talk to you, if you want to come over, but I really understand if you don't."

The whole situation was like a scab you know you should leave alone but can't help picking at. I agreed to go to Melissa's apartment and meet Lennox.

"Apartment" probably conjures up somewhere more fancy than Melissa's place. It's an upstairs unit in an old wooden house divided into four. The best thing about it is the beautiful old trees which screen it from the road and wrap it in green coolness. There are other semi-modern, brick units in the street and a few detached homes. Just around the corner, the traffic heading for the centre of Southport flashes past in a regular stream. Inside Melissa had draped fabrics and thrown rugs which more or less hid the tired furnishings and thin carpet. Open windows and glossy leaves give the impression of being in a tree house.

Lennox, confident-looking, curly-haired and angular, was sitting in an old cane chair strumming a guitar.

He put down the guitar and stood up when Melissa introduced us.

"Hi Hannah. I can see the family resemblance. Melissa darl, how about a drink?"

"Ginger beer?"

"She's such a health freak, this is the nearest I get to alcohol." He laughed and put a possessive arm around her slender shoulders. "Ginger beer okay for you, Hannah?"

"Yes, thanks."

"Come and sit down," he said, patting the floral throw on the sofa. He sat beside me, and Melissa sat in the cane chair. "We are all shocked about Daniel," he continued after a long swig from the bottle. "He seemed like a friendly enough guy. We played guitar together once but I didn't know him well."

"Were you there when Jessica was shot?"

"I heard the shots and that was it. After a few seconds it was chaos — people running everywhere."

"Why did you all leave?"

"I guess we panicked and decided to go before the shit hit the fan. Two of the women stayed with Jessica until the ambulance came, but I instructed everyone else to leave and stay silent if the police caught up with them. It was very important that this "incident" wasn't allowed to get in the way of The Poet's vision. The simplest answer was to lie low until the fuss died down. Or at least it would have been if the media hadn't invented their own version of things."

"And the police didn't catch up with you?"

"We knew the police would come out from the north so we went over the border into New South Wales in people's cars and the mini-bus. The cops were too slow to catch a cold."

"So where is everyone now?"

"Those who could afford it have gone to India. The Poet is supposed to be stopping off there on his way back from looking for a commune site in Europe."

"And Daniel?"

"Don't know where he and Casey went. Or where they are now. I'm keeping a low profile myself. That's why I couldn't visit Melissa for a while. The cops may have a file on me because a paranoid ex-girlfriend thought I was stalking her once and got a restraining order against me. Keeping out of their way is one of my priorities at the best of times."

"And you think Daniel did it?"

"It all points to him, doesn't it? Melissa, this beer is warm. Is something wrong with the fridge?"

"It hasn't been in the fridge. It's too 'yin' for me if I keep it in the fridge."

"You have to understand, Hannah, that not everyone can live up to the ideals of someone like The Poet. We're all masters of our own destiny but we're infected by this sick society."

I nodded uncertainly.

"Lennox is so strong and so clear in his perceptions," Melissa said with an admiring glance at him.

"I have found a very sensitive woman, here," Lennox said, touching Melissa's knee. "There aren't many people with the imagination to see beyond the conventions that bind us."

Despite Lennox's self-assured arrogance, I could see what Melissa found attractive in him. He's one of those people who look into your eyes with such concentration when they're speaking that you feel both important and a little uncomfortable. I found I didn't want to disagree with anything he said. That penetrating gaze seemed to probe and challenge at once, and held on to me even after he finished speaking. I was always the one who looked away first. He did the same with Melissa, but I saw her eyes melt into calm pools when his laser beams fixed on her.

"Did you know Jessica? Why would Daniel want to hurt her?"

"She's an ex-girlfriend of mine. Pretty girl. Daniel had the hots for her, I know that much."

"But he was going out with Jody!"

He looked at me as if my comment was too naive for serious consideration.

"Let's just say Jessica knew how to use her body as bait. The Poet talked about love but most people have no idea what that means." His eyes burned the message into mine.

"Another ginger beer?" Melissa offered.

Lennox dismissed the offer with a raised hand. "You're a great kid, Hannah," he said. "Don't slide into the superficial ways of this world." His compliment was delivered with the same focused strength as his pronouncements on life. Although I bristled at being called "kid", his approval was worth having.

"Lennox has *such* high ideals," Melissa said. "… and he's right, of course. It's easy to get conditioned by our materialistic society."

I left Melissa's feeling deflated and colourless. I envied her and Lennox's certainty and shared purpose. My life was a frayed and tangled mess in comparison.

THIRTEEN

I watched the farmers on TV, standing thigh-deep in water where only last year they stood beside sun-baked carcasses of drought-stricken cattle. I heard their despair as they were left to their fate — banks, government and dreams deserting them. Like them, I seemed to be at the mercy of forces I couldn't control. If God was a ten-pin bowler, he'd have scored a strike with the ball of events that came rumbling towards us this year.

Everything had been eerily quiet for five weeks since I visited Lennox and Melissa. No word from them or from Jody. No news on TV or from the police. No more dates with Sam. There was a rumour that he'd asked Bianca out, but she said no because she'd seen porn pictures in his locker. I was almost getting used to the idea that I might not see Daniel for a very long time.

The summer seemed to be having a last blast before it burnt itself out. Even my fingertips were sweaty when I reached my hand through the tresses of magenta bougainvillea to pull the letters from our mail box. Among the usual bundle of bills and hardware catalogues, there was a pale blue aerogram.

The flimsy folded paper came from India and I didn't

recognise the handwriting, but it was addressed to me. I turned it over. The sender was Casey Phipps, c/o GPO Mahaban, Maharastra, India.

I don't often get letters but, when I do, I have to sit down and read them with proper ceremony. Although I was curious, I first took an icy orange juice from the fridge and a knife from the kitchen drawer. Then I closed my bedroom door and carefully slit the aerogram open. Inside, the writing was Daniel's.

Hi Hannah,

Would you believe I'm in India? Well you probably would from the stamps and postmark but I can hardly believe it myself! I'll put Casey's name on the back of this letter in case the police are watching our mail (am I being paranoid?).

I just wanted you (and Mum and Dad) to know I'm okay. At least I'm okay-ish. I've sold some stuff (guitar etc.) to get here and Casey's helped me with a long-term loan. Living is really cheap so I'll be able to stay a while.

I don't know how to start explaining everything to you. For now, please believe I didn't shoot Jessica. I know it looks as if I did with my fingerprints on the gun, but there's more to the story than I can prove at the moment.

India is one strange place but I'm getting to like it. You'd love the light and colour — there's a photo opportunity every few metres.

Hope you're all well. Don't worry about me.

You can write to the Poste Restante address if you like.

Love, Daniel

I read it two or three times. Perhaps the shock and the heat had got to me but I started to laugh. Our Daniel had made it out of the country.

I had to wait an hour for Mum to get home before I could tell her. "Where?" she exclaimed in a voice that told me she'd heard right the first time. I repeated it.

"India. Maha-somwhere-or-other. Look." Since I'd read the letter, my initial relief that Daniel had escaped the police, and the glimmer of hope that perhaps he wasn't guilty after all, had changed to more questions. How had he got out of the country if the police were looking for him? What would happen when their money ran out and they had to come home? They were questions Mum asked too after she'd taken in the news.

"I can't believe he'd go to India! He's only ever been on the school trip to Vanuatu." She turned the jug on. She always has a cup of tea when she gets in from work and she had hardly got through the door when I'd told her the news.

"You weren't much older when you went travelling, were you?"

"Only a couple of years, I suppose. But I wasn't on the run from the police."

"What do you think Dad will say?"

"I don't know. He doesn't want to hear about Daniel at the moment. I think he feels Daniel's problems reflect on him. And he's always hated situations where he's powerless to do anything. But we'll have to tell him." She put a low-caffeine tea bag in a mug, changed her mind and put a full-strength one in instead.

"I'm going to write straight back. At least we know where he is now."

"I suppose we should tell the police."

"No, Mum. They'll extradite him."

The jug got noisier as it progressed towards the boil. "A trial should find out the truth." She looked doubtful. "But I wouldn't really want him to have to go through that."

"If Daniel was a danger to people, I guess we would have to tell the police, but, even if he did it, it could have been an accident or something."

"I wonder if the police would bother to extradite him from India? He's not exactly a major criminal."

"We can't chance it. Don't tell them, Mum."

"You're probably right." The jug boiled and turned itself off with a click. "But I'll have to see what your father says."

"Do we have to tell Dad?"

"Of course." She poured the water and churned the tea bag around in the mug. "Imagine how angry he'd be if we didn't tell him." She spooned two heaps of sugar into her tea. She never used to take any.

"Imagine how angry he'll be when you do tell him!"

But Dad only stared at the letter and shook his head.

The following day, I was in trouble at school for missing an assignment deadline. I just couldn't concentrate. I was beginning to think I'd have to repeat the year, which made me feel even more depressed.

And I found out that Sam had started dating Leilani. Leilani with the long legs, long hair and long list of boyfriends.

I'd intended to work on my latest geography assignment when I got home, but Daniel's letter was demanding the mind-space. I began my reply two or three times before I managed to pen the words down in roughly the right order.

Dear Daniel,
I was so surprised to get your letter! We're glad to hear you're still alive! It's been awful since the shooting. The worst thing has been not being able to talk to you …

After all this time, it was difficult to know whether to be serious or flippant, whether I was writing to a suspect on the run or a tourist in India. The end result was a schizophrenic mixture.

I posted the letter and postponed the geography.

It was one of those warm evenings in front of a mediocre TV program when you know you ought to go and do something else but somehow you can't quite find the energy to break free of your lethargy. A heavyweight cicada was making its deep, vibrating call just outside the window. Mum waltzed into the room looking unusually perky.

"Come and talk to us in the kitchen," she commanded. "Dad has a suggestion."

With a flick of the remote control, the predictable people existed no more.

Even Dad looked as if a weight had lifted from his head and shoulders. "Your mother and I are going to India for a fortnight to see what's going on with Daniel. Do you think one of your friend's parents could put you up while we're away?"

I looked at each of them in turn. "When did you decide this?"

"This evening," Dad said. "I've been thinking about it since you got that letter. I decided we've got to do something."

"It'll take a bit of arranging," Mum added. "But I'm due for some holidays. We'll find out tomorrow how long it'll take to get the visas and we'll book to go as soon as possible."

"Can't I come too?"

"You've got school, Hannah. This is a vital year for you. And there's no point in all of us going." Mum sounded unusually decisive.

"I can catch up. If we go soon, it would be mostly Easter holidays anyway. And there's no one I can stay with. Tori's mum doesn't allow sleepovers on school days and I think they're going to Western Australia during the break. I want to come with you. Think of the experience. It's more educational than a hundred geography text books!"

"You'd probably hate it. It's not the Sunshine Coast, you know. It won't be a *holiday*."

"I know, Mum. I could help you find Daniel. You've got to let me come. I couldn't bear to be left here."

"It's an extra expense —" Mum began.

"Things are really cheap in India, Daniel said in his letter. It could be my birthday present in advance."

Mum looked at Dad.

"She *could* come," Dad said to Mum, "if she can find a way to reschedule the schoolwork. I guess a totally different culture is relevant to her studies."

From that moment I knew I was going to India. And Dad gave me a half-smile that told me, despite everything, that he might enjoy having me as part of the family adventure.

FOURTEEN

Everything went even more crazy the next couple of weeks. I can't remember ever seeing Mum more excited. She went dashing round the shops collecting clothes from the summer sales, like someone on a manic treasure hunt. A Panama hat that looked as if it should be worn by a tiger hunter replaced her raffia hat. She called it her "Memsahib hat". The arguments between her and Dad had stopped. Not that they were being affectionate, but when Dad criticised her over-spending or frantic activity, there was an almost-friendly acceptance in his voice.

I phoned Jody and told her that we were going. She made me promise to come to Brisbane before we left and collect some things she wanted me to take to Daniel. "I'll get him a couple of good books and some decent sunnies. He'll have glaucoma by the time he's twenty-five if he doesn't wear them over there. You're so lucky to be going! You rich kids have it made."

"I'm not a rich kid," I protested. "Mum and Dad both work and we've never had an overseas holiday before."

"You're rich compared with me. It'll take some scrimping to get sunnies for Daniel. I'm working in the petrol station in the evenings now. D'you think Danny would like sunnies or have you got any other ideas? Will you have room to take the kimono I bought in Byron?"

I decided to buy a suitcase one size bigger than I'd need for my own stuff. And in between the preparations, I started writing this story of Daniel. Not so much "Daniel in the Lion's Den" but maybe "Daniel in The Poet's Den".

It was good to get away for the day with Jody. We met at Southbank and sat near the Nepalese pagodas watching boats chug up and down the Brisbane river. The mirrored windows of the city towers captured the vivid sky and distorted ivory clouds mixing them with concrete, sandstone and brick. The numbers of a digital clock on one building counted the minutes in neon red. Just across the river, an old boat with palms on the deck was filling with party people.

"Don't you just love this city!" Jody said. "Where else have you got all this?" It was a rhetorical question, of course. "I wonder what the weather's like in India at this time of year? Do you think you'll find Daniel easily when you get there?"

"Mum says it'll be spring. Hot days. Might be cool in the early morning and evening. We don't know how difficult it'll be to find him. We wrote to him and told him when we'll be arriving and gave him a time and place to meet us in Bombay. We don't even know if he'll come. And what if he's moved on? Imagine trying to find them in all those hundreds of millions of people."

"Worse than the Gabba at a test match! You'll find him — if Its-Supreme-Mysteriousness wishes. Do you think he still cares about me — Daniel I mean?"

"Of course. What's this 'Supreme Mysteriousness'?"

"It's what we called 'God' or 'The power that makes things tick'. It's sort of like 'His Royal Highness' but it can't be a 'Him' or a 'Her' if it's formless. 'Its-Supreme-Mysteriousness' is kind of good, eh?"

We bought some slices of pizza from a cheap and cheerful takeaway with white plastic tables and scraped our chairs into the shade of the green and white striped umbrella. I showed Jody the photos I took in Byron Bay and she made me promise to give Daniel the three best ones of her.

Then she walked back to the station with me. "I'd give anything to come to India with you," she said. "Tell Danny to come home soon. Tell him I miss him, if you think he's missing me." She stared into the distance of some imagined past or future. "No, tell him I miss him *anyway*. And take heaps of photos — you're really good with a camera."

I watched her walk back towards the bridge, a lonely figure, smaller than I usually think of her, which soon dissolved into shifting pools of people.

Now there were only a few days before departure. I phoned Melissa and told her I was going. She sounded surprised, then showered me with reassurances of what a wonderful experience it would be. She wanted to know whereabouts in India the guys were staying and said she'd heard that a few other members of the Tribe had gathered in Mahaban. Mahaban had apparently been an important place in The Poet's history — the story was that he'd spent two years there meditating before he'd had the insights which changed his life forever. Then we received a brief aerogram from Daniel: *I'll meet you all at the Raj Hotel, Bombay, at 4 pm on 23rd April.*

FIFTEEN

Lines of people with luggage at their sides shuffled along to the check-in counters. There were people in smart suits, others in jeans, one plump guy in a tracksuit, Indian women in saris and a blond-haired model-type in a jacaranda matt silk jumpsuit. There was a little Indian girl in a pink party dress with satin ribbons in thick black hair. She hid behind her mother when I looked at her, then peeped out shyly. I was beginning to feel like a traveller already and this was only Brisbane airport.

My parents suddenly looked like people who knew what they were doing. Dad was wearing comfortable khaki pants and almost-matching jacket. As well as his rather old brown suitcase, he had a small canvas backpack that looked as if it dated back to his army days. He herded me into the cordoned-off queue and organised our tickets and passports ready to present at the check-in. Mum had bought new rather baggy white pants, which I thought might have been a mistake as she's not as slender as she used to be, but they looked exotic with a long plum-coloured top and a dangly scarf. She was checking her watch and telling us we'd have plenty of time for a drink and a look round the shops before we needed to go through to "Departures".

"I think we all needed this break," Mum said, as we sat with our drinks in what could have been mistaken for a trendy city café except that we were looking across the top of indoor trees to an expanse of runway beyond the towering glass wall. The distant Pacific light unrolled across the mud-flats and the tarmac.

"It'll be a holiday of sorts, if nothing else," Dad replied with a certain grimness of expression.

"Just ten hours and we'll be in India," Mum commented as she pushed her cappuccino cup aside to fill in the departure card. I could tell she was as excited as a kid but too sensible to show it.

"Ten and a half. For better or worse," said Dad.

I wished I could have done this journey with Daniel. That would really have been an adventure.

My spirits lifted with the 5000-tonne jumbo. It was equally hard to believe that either could soar so easily. The frustrations of the last few months were being left behind along with the clusters of minuscule buildings, both suddenly insignificant in the expanded landscape.

My eyes skimmed the relief map spread out below in every direction like crumpled brown fabric. Then the flight attendant asked me to close the window cover for the movie and I reluctantly exchanged my omnipresence for ninety minutes of gang warfare amidst the tenements of New York. By the time our heroes were shot, stabbed or fatally overdosed, the distant clouds were heavily saturated with pink and the land had a transient glow before disappearing into darkness. For a while we chased the last remnants of cerise and saffron towards the west.

Night merged into more night until we seemed suspended in a place where time doesn't move. Somewhere in the midst of a dream, we were herded from our sleepy capsule onto Indian ground. The air was warm and thick and permeated with strange smells. Aviation fuel and a land exhaling unfamiliar life odours. I imagined I could identify spices and sour vegetation but they were only two in a concoction that was simultaneously sweet and slightly sickening.

We seemed to swim in a dreamlike sea of dark faces, struggling with luggage, waiting in lines. There were too many people moving in meaningless patterns, pushing, shoving, bumping, staring. A man in a turban was talking to Dad. It all became a blur for me. I was only aware of waiting zombie-like for our passports to be inspected, for forms to be filled and for our luggage to be cleared by a surly man who took no heed of the hundreds queuing, and suspiciously opened most people's bags, baring their contents to the crowds. It was hours after we landed, but still part of the endless, smudged night, when we sped in a yellow and black taxi through a baffling landscape of indecipherable signs, unhealthy-looking buildings and unfamiliar shadows. I stared at corpse-like lumps on the pavement. "People sleeping," Mum whispered.

I closed my eyes and wished for a comfortable hotel.

The first grey and pink daylight was rising from the pavements as we stopped outside an old, white-painted building. Matching fortress-like walls with irregular spears of broken glass embedded in the top surrounded the small palm-filled garden, and a young Indian in a white jacket and pants stood guard beside the narrow gateway. In the dawn dimness it looked like a tinted black and white photo from another era.

A skinny dog with only three legs scuttled along sniffing the base of the wall, and looming out of the twilight came a creaky old cart, piled high with vegetation and pulled by an enormous pale Brahmin bull. A crinkled old man sat crouched at the front of cart and stared unsmiling into the distance. As I opened the car door I nearly hit a guy on a bicycle with no lights who was gliding silently past. In the doorway of the building opposite the hotel a murky turquoise bundle lay sleeping against the grey security shutters.

I breathed in the spicy, cool air laced with layers of mystery and the faint undertones of rotting garbage. The dull buzz of scooter taxis darting about could be heard at the end of the street, and the distant traffic noise was frequently punctuated by "beep-beep" from horns.

"The city never sleeps," said Dad in a half whisper as we trudged up the few broad steps through a pillared entrance and into the doorless reception area of the hotel. As if to prove him wrong, an old man was asleep on a leather sofa in the foyer and there was no one at the reception desk.

Dad rang the bell and a young woman emerged from a back room, straightening her sari as if she too might have been sleeping.

"Two rooms for Jarvis. We booked," Dad said.

She looked down a long sheet of paper and nodded. "Not two rooms together. Only having two rooms separate. Maybe tomorrow two rooms adjoining."

"Hannah will be okay," Mum reassured Dad. "You don't need to be under our noses, do you Hannah?"

For one stupid moment I felt scared of being alone in this place. "I'll be fine, wherever," I said. A faded blue sign behind the desk said "Welcome Hotel Chandra. All rooms with bathrooms. Management requests quiet after 9 pm. Check-out not after 11 am".

The receptionist gave us our keys and shouted something in a surprisingly sharp and commanding voice. The old man rose hurriedly from the sofa and came to take our luggage. I felt sorry for him; his sinewy brown wrists protruding from a white tunic looked strained with the weight of our bags, but he smiled and shuffled ahead of us, badly fitting plastic sandals hardly lifting from the floor. The lift lurched up a couple of floors and we were shown to our rooms. "See you downstairs at nine. We'll get breakfast together," Dad said.

I'd expected to fall asleep immediately, but the strangeness of India seeped through the closed shutters and, though I closed my eyes, the increasing volume of the day outside kept me drifting half-awake. Gradually the cacophony blurred into a background soundscape and I slept for a while. When I woke, I opened the shutters and saw my first technicolour diorama of India.

My window looked down on a narrow back street behind the hotel. A golden-faced Indian woman stared at me from a massive blue poster across the street. There were two guys in the background of her life and, though I couldn't read the tapeworm words, I could imagine the movie. Dwarfed below her, real life was crazier, dirtier, more desperate, but no less colourful. Old women and young women, in vivid uninhibited hues only slightly subdued by dirt and wear, were sitting cross-legged or squatting beside their goods for sale. Each had just one or two pyramid piles to sell — red chillies and lemons, or small clusters of bananas, or rather mottled mangoes and a few potatoes. Behind them, open-fronted shops like up-ended shoeboxes had sacks of lentils, spices, rice and unfamiliar beans, all collecting the dust and debris from the street. Indians of every shape and size were tracing erratic paths, creating a constantly moving mass the width of the narrow thoroughfare. Schools of bicycles rang their bells constantly and, although ignored, managed to weave a way through the pedestrians. An occasional motor-scooter rickshaw navigated through the crowds, sending furious fumes over the food. In the midst of it all, a caramel-coloured cow stood eating a pile of half-mulched leaves and stalks.

A knock on my door and Mum's voice told me it was already nine-fifteen. She said they'd check out breakfast possibilities and come back in half an hour when I'd showered.

The bathroom was primitive but had two toilets — one ancient throne with a high cistern and chain, the other a tiled hole in the ground with convenient foot holds for squatting. I stood gingerly under the shower which gurgled and coughed a bit before giving an ungenerous spurt of lukewarm water. At least it was wet and fresh.

"Don't you just love this place?" Mum asked as we sat, lone diners in the hotel's restaurant which looked out onto the central courtyard where a gardener lazily hosed the greenery in a shaft of sunlight.

"It's unusual," I said, humouring her.

"You'll get used to it," Dad said to me.

"Are we the only ones staying here?" I asked. "I haven't seen any other guests yet."

"Everyone else had breakfast hours ago," Dad said. This is the only restaurant around here that does western breakfasts, but we can go out for lunch or dinner."

"What are we going to do today?"

"Explore!" said Mum. "Let's get a taxi downtown and see what we can see!"

"That means at least half an hour sitting in traffic fumes in the heat," Dad said between mouthfuls of toast. I wish he wouldn't dampen Mum's sparks of enthusiasm.

"It's no distance," said Mum looking at the map in her guidebook. "And we might as well enjoy ourselves. We've got two days before we meet Daniel and there's nothing else we can do about him until then." Mum spread another piece of toast with a determined stroke of her knife.

"You should have arranged that sooner," Dad said. "We're here to find Daniel and bring him home, remember?"

I had a horrible feeling Daniel wouldn't be so easy to "bring home". I dismissed the thought from my mind.

SIXTEEN

Two days is a long time in India. The slightly disoriented travel-haze merged into a feeling of living in a warm, vivid dream. New sounds, sights, smells spiralled and tugged, jostled and mesmerised. One moment the explosion of colour, noise and vibrant aliveness would fascinate and stimulate; the next moment poverty or filth would contaminate the scene and leave an aftertaste of anger or disbelief. Patterns of people, vehicles, bicycles and skinny animals constantly shifted into new arrangements like the swirling of a flooded river.

From my window I watched a young woman, probably no older than me, sitting with her toddler amongst the dirt and debris of the market. Sometimes he fed at her breast; sometimes she picked through his hair for lice; sometimes he crawled amongst the vegetables and sucked on a discarded fruit. She was an efficient mother (discounting hygiene!), alert and no-nonsense with the people who haggled for bananas, confidently in control of the things she could control and seeming to accept the rest. She was slender, economical but graceful in her movements, and her dusty skin glowed against the faded berry-coloured sari she wore every day. It wouldn't be entirely accurate to say I envied her, but watching her made me aware of an uncomfortable gap in myself.

The hotel where we were going to meet Daniel was about twenty minutes walk from where we were staying but Mum insisted we take a taxi. "We can't arrive there sweaty and dirty," she said. She'd also instructed us to dress in something "more elegant" than our sightseeing clothes. I put on my long wrap-around skirt with some Indian sandals I'd bought the day before and a short T-shirt. Dad was worried that it didn't meet the top of the skirt, but Mum pointed out that saris leave an expanse of midriff and I'd fit right in.

We were all a bit edgy that morning. None of us said it but I knew we were wondering if Daniel would show up. A wasted trip to Byron Bay was one thing, but a wasted trip to India would be something too enormous to contemplate.

After the heat and noise of the streets, the interior of the Raj was cool and quiet. Marble floors, high ceilings and sandalwood-scented air spoke of palaces and grand princes, English ladies of another era in sweeping dresses, and a time when people might have arrived on ornately decorated elephants rather than in taxis.

We found the first-floor restaurant with a view of the Gateway of India and a rather murky-looking Arabian Sea. It was ten minutes before the time we'd arranged to meet Daniel. I ordered *Limca* (sweet, lemon, fizzy), Mum had chai and Dad had coffee. We looked at each other and looked out of the window. Mum made a couple of attempts to start a conversation but she couldn't get one off the ground. Immaculately uniformed waiters glided swiftly to serve the few other guests. Very different from our shuffling friend at the Chandra Hotel. At a nearby table, two older ladies with English accents, fair skinned in faded floral dresses, were having proper tea from a teapot (not the sweet milky chai in little glasses that Mum drinks everywhere). I guessed they were teachers.

Dad scratched at a little flaw on his saucer. Mum kept smoothing her hair. I twirled the straw in my Limca.

Then he came. He was suddenly beside us; a slender young man in rather crumpled chinos and an open-necked white cheesecloth shirt. "Mrs Jarvis?" he asked, catching Mum's eye first.

"Yes. Are you Casey?" Mum looked beyond him and around the restaurant. "Where's Daniel?"

"Daniel couldn't make it."

"Couldn't make it?" Instant devastation was obvious in Mum's face and voice.

"Can we talk?"

"Sit down." We all stood up and shuffled our chairs around uneasily.

Dad shook Casey's hand rather formally and said, "G'Day Casey. I'm Martin Jarvis. This is my wife, Nicole, and Daniel's sister, Hannah." Casey sat opposite me and gave me half a smile. He looked a little apprehensive but self-contained. Slightly sun-bleached, curly hair was not too tame and not too wild. Faint freckles misted golden skin.

There was an awkward pause. None of us knew where to start.

"Did you have a good journey here?" Mum asked.

"Not bad. I always enjoy the Indian trains. Where are you guys staying?"

"The Chandra Hotel. It's an old place about twenty minutes away. Not as grand as this." Mum seemed to be our spokesperson.

"This is cool, eh? Your first visit to India?"

"No, I was here for a few weeks, years back. Not long before I met Martin. We met in Vietnam and sometimes things here remind me ..."

A waiter came and Casey ordered *Campa Cola*. We had a repeat round of drinks.

"Coca-Cola and Pepsi were banned in India until fairly

recently. They had it right, I reckon. Why let the multinationals take all the profits when you're a struggling third-world country? I still support the local product." Casey paused. "You are not a Coca-Cola executive, I hope?" he asked Dad. His afterthought lightened the atmosphere between us a little. I liked the way he was right in there, keeping the communication flowing.

"No. I have a computer business." I looked at Dad and wondered how Casey saw him. For a moment my familiar father was a stranger to me too. I saw someone kind of stiff and defensive. Someone who had shut the world out long ago. And shut himself in. I switched back to my usual view of him. Just Dad. Too inclined to do the "heavy father" number but keen to sing our praises in public. Often distant but always there. "So what's the story with Daniel?"

"I don't know quite how to tell you this, but he doesn't want to see you at the moment. He said to say he'll come and visit you when he gets back to Australia."

It took a moment to digest. "This is ridiculous!" Dad said. "He must have been brainwashed!"

"He knows exactly what he's doing, Mr Jarvis. But he's concerned you might have planned a kidnap attempt."

"Kidnap?"

"I guess you've heard about the parents' group that has been forcibly 'rescuing' their children from The New Tribe?" Casey asked.

"We only want to see him and talk to him," said Mum, "We wouldn't force him into anything."

"I'm sorry. I know you've come a long way but it's his decision. He did say Hannah could visit us for a few days. I would escort her there and back, if you agree."

"Out of the question," Dad said.

"I can't believe he won't see us when we've come all this way! I just want to talk to him." Tears were welling up in Mum's eyes.

"I'm sorry," said Casey.

"Can I phone him and talk to him? I know I could reassure him that we're not going to force him into anything," Mum pleaded.

"I'll take your phone number at the hotel and ask him to call you."

"Can't I go with Casey?" I asked. "I could find out how he is and everything. Maybe I could persuade him to see you."

"Absolutely not," Dad said.

"I'd be fine. You treat me like a child!"

"No. And don't raise your voice. We don't want a scene here."

I was angry but I didn't want a scene either. I didn't want to look a fool in front of Casey.

"Perhaps I should be going," Casey said. "I'm staying in Bombay overnight. You can still contact me if you want to." He stood up and handed Mum a card that said Delite Hotel.

"Don't go. Please finish your drink," Mum said in her most unrefusable voice. "This business with Daniel has been hard for all of us."

Casey glanced at Dad. "No need to rush off," Dad said gruffly.

"Enjoying India, Hannah?" Casey's question changed the subject as gracefully as possible in the circumstances.

"Yes. And no. More yes, I think, now I'm getting used to it."

"Good answer," he said. "I give India an almighty 'yes' and an almighty 'no' too. Depends which day you ask me." I was reeled in and held by his smile.

"Do you think Daniel is innocent?" I asked Casey as everyone drained the last of their drinks.

They all looked at me.

"I'd bet my life on it." He smiled as if I was right to have brought the subject up. "But you should hear his story from him. The truth must come out eventually, but at the moment it's his word against someone else's."

"Against whose?" Mum was quickest with the obvious question.

"He won't tell us that."

"Why didn't they stop Daniel at the airport? I would have thought the police would have had people's names in the computer these days." Mum rubbed her finger round the rim of her chai glass.

"We thought of that. We'd got friendly with some boaties down in New South Wales and there was a couple that wanted a crew to New Zealand. I did some sailing at school and they were happy to take us. Daniel was seasick all the way, which he started to think was some sort of divine retribution for fleeing the country. But once we were back on dry land, the pressure was off and we flew out from Auckland."

"Is The Poet here in India?" I suddenly felt confident to let some of the stored-up questions spill out.

"We think so but we haven't seen him yet."

"Who is this guy? The Poet?" Dad almost spat the question.

"He's a very simple guy who searched for truth for a number of years. He talks a heap of sense."

"Not what I'd call sense." Dad looked close to boiling point.

"Here's our phone number at the hotel." Mum had been writing on a scrap of paper. "When will you be able to give it to him?"

"I'll be back there tomorrow."

"And tell him it's time he woke up to himself. We've come halfway round the bloody world to see him," Dad growled.

"He needs your support ..." Casey began.

"Then why the hell isn't he here to see us?" Dad's explosive anger propelled him away from the table. "You'll have to excuse me. I think I've picked up a stomach bug." He marched away without looking back.

"Sorry, Casey," Mum said. "I'd better go after him. Are you coming, Hannah?"

I hesitated.

"I'll see Hannah back later, if you like," Casey said. "It would give us time to talk a bit more." He was looking to both Mum and me for agreement.

I nodded.

"We want all the news of Daniel," Mum said. "You've got money for the taxi, Hannah?"

"Don't worry, I'll take care of her," Casey said before I could reply. "I've been looking forward to meeting your family," he continued when Mum had gone.

"Sorry about Dad." I sighed.

"Daniel told me what to expect. He's not that bad. More Limca?"

On the way back to the hotel, Casey impressed me by giving the taxi driver instructions in Hindi. The only few words he knew, he said. He paid the taxi driver and got out with me. "I'll walk the last bit. Every street is an adventure around here." We watched the taxi do a U-turn, almost obliterating a guy on a bicycle, then, just when I thought he was about to walk out of my life the same day he'd walked into it, he said, "Would you like to eat with me tonight? I know an excellent little Indian restaurant!"

"Sure. An Indian restaurant would be perfect!"

"I'll meet you here at six-thirty."

SEVENTEEN

Mum and Dad hadn't shown up back at the hotel before I went out so I left them a note to tell them I'd gone out with Casey.

"Happy to walk? It's only about ten minutes " Casey's smile would have made a ten-hour walk seem a casual stroll.

He led the way through narrow streets, everywhere blazing with lights, as busy and bright as a Christmas Eve shopping spree. Once or twice he took my hand to stop me getting separated from him as we wove through dense clumps of crowd. His hand was warm, dry, smooth. A guy with a barrow full of fruit, beneath a glaring naked light bulb, was creating wondrous juices. He smiled at me and called out "Mango juice. First class mango juice. Best mango juice." The ripe mango smell mixed with smoke from an old man's beedi and the ever-present mist of spiciness. An unfamiliar song wailed from the juice wallah's cassette player competing with the murmur of the crowd and the background of constant city traffic horns. Glistening, syrup-dipped, crispy-fried sweets, in circles and figure-of-eight shapes, hung like distorted orange icicles on another barrow. In a paint-splattered alcove, a statue was garlanded with marigolds and jasmine. Children turned and stared at us with curious dark eyes. The night stood back from it all.

"Okay?" Casey was bright with the light, high on the carnival chaos. I could tell. I was too.

"Great."

We walked, skipped and side-stepped onwards, specks on the colour-splattered canvas of a crazy artist. When sensory saturation sets in you either shut down or spiral up. We spiralled.

A girl, only five or six, with smeared face and tangled hair, tugged my shirt and held out a pleading hand. "Paise, paise? Whatisyourname? Paise?" Casey took 50 paise from his pocket and gave it to her.

"Now run!" he said to me, grabbing my hand to drag me. In the next street he slowed and looked behind. "We did it! Usually if you give to one, a crowd of others appear from nowhere."

By the time we slipped into the relative calm of the restaurant I felt as if we'd climbed a mountain together. A sort of exhilarated, satisfied, close-to-laughter, post-adrenalin high.

"Amazing, eh?" Casey murmured as our focus returned to each other.

"It's unbelievable! Like the offspring of a medieval fayre and an electronics showroom!"

"Aha! India has bitten you now. Your blood is infected. I'm not sure whether it's virus or elixir but I see it in your eyes!"

"Is that what makes *your* eyes shine?" Surely this wasn't me, flirting so obviously.

"Perhaps they shine when they like what they see." His expression challenged me. "Some enchanted evening, eh?" He studied his menu for a moment. "I recommend the marsala dosas here. Or the dahi vada. Or malai kofta. Shall we get a selection and share?"

"Sure. You choose. You seem to be an expert after your couple of months in India."

"Never trust an expert!"

"I'll trust you — on this occasion."

"Mad woman!"

"I thought you'd be more serious than you are. You know, because you're in a religious cult and all that stuff."

"I couldn't be serious all the time! But we can talk about Life-and-the-Meaning-of-the-Universe and Everything if you want."

"I wouldn't know where to begin."

"Are you interested?"

"What, in religious stuff? Not really. The questions are too big and how can you know if any of the answers people tell you are right?"

"Aha, that's the challenge."

"You don't seem like someone who would be in a cult."

"The word 'cult' has all the wrong connotations. You have to realise that all the major religions started as cults. Even Kelloggs cornflakes were invented for the vegetarian diet of Seventh Day Adventists who, at that time, were a cult in America. Bet you didn't know that! I'm a mine of useless information. But for me it's just about feeling at home. About hearing someone who's actually original. It's like an oasis in a desert. I never thought of myself as religious, but I respect The Poet because he's been out there learning as he lived. Who else can you really respect? People get older but most of them don't get any wiser."

"How about doctors? Scientists who make things better in the world? Can't you respect them?"

"Doctors look after our bodies, sure. And some of the things science has given us are useful. But don't you ever yearn for something more *real*? Something you can't even explain? There's no one to look after our spirit these days. Religions and myth are on the scrap heap because science has 'proved' them wrong. But science is just as much a 'belief system' — you have to believe only what can be logically proved from our current point in evolution. It really comes down to whether you believe that all this — all this amazing life and its intricately balanced systems — is just a mechanical accident or whether you know there has to be some intelligence — and I don't mean a bearded man in the sky — behind it all."

"Well —"

"Hey, I don't want to sound like a preacher. You'll think I'm trying to convert you."

"I think I could be converted tonight! I feel as if I've lost the usual me, here in India."

"Excellent! Isn't it an adventure to flow along with the current and see where it takes us?"

I hardly needed to agree when an uncontrollable smile kept taking over my mouth. "How did you get involved with the Tribe, anyway?"

"A friend at uni. I dropped out of my second year, last year. I was doing psychology. I'd still like to be a psychologist but I want to live a bit first. The work was getting tough. Either the living or the course had to go. Visits to Miralee were just going to be *part* of living, but then I found I didn't really want to be anywhere else."

"What was the big attraction?"

"The Poet of course. Did you ever think in religion lessons that you would have followed Jesus if you'd been living in his time? I did. And then someone comes along who speaks with real wisdom and you just *know* what the disciples left home for. I also feel privileged to be part of this experiment in humanity's evolution."

"Experiment?"

"An increase in consciousness. Living in harmony with nature. We're trying to use the best of the modern world without being materialistic. You know, the more we focus on competing for what we want, the more we isolate ourselves. You have to hear The Poet explain it."

"It doesn't sound *too* weird when you explain it. Are they really just ordinary people who join?"

"Am I ordinary? Is Daniel ordinary? Is Jody ordinary? I guess you can't be *too* ordinary! And I have to admit there were a few weirdos there. I suppose most of us were people that were hungry for something."

"Including you?"

"Sure. When Dad died something changed for me. You can't watch someone you love and admire gradually disintegrate before your eyes and not be changed. It's hard to care what happens in *Home and Away* when your father is lying in bed, bald from chemo, frightened. He'd always been strong. He played tennis for Queensland when he was younger. There was really no one who could answer my deepest questions about life. I was ready to hear someone like The Poet but I'm no fool. You have to keep exploring, finding your own answers. I was chief of Cynics Corner at Miralee but I love The Poet. There's a different quality about an enlightened person."

"Enlightened?"

"You know, like the Buddha. He's no longer attached to all the things of the world."

"Is that good? Not being attached, I mean. Not caring about anything sounds incredibly boring and inhuman."

"It's the only way we can be free. Let's face it, most of what we call caring about each other is wanting to get something for ourselves. If we get past our own ulterior motives, we can respond to what others really need. And you couldn't meet a more compassionate person than The Poet."

"I'm not sure I entirely understand."

In an exaggerated Indian accent he said, "Takes many, many years. Maybe many, many lifetimes. We are not achieving total understanding in one evening!" Then, in normal Casey voice, "Hey, let's eat! Too much talking!"

Warmth of spices. Warmth of Indian evening. Warmth of eyes and smiles. Zest of ginger. Fire of chilli. My feet were way off the ground and I didn't care if I never put them down again.

"Try this lassi." Casey handed me his milky-looking drink.

"Lassi! Sounds like something you feed to the Rottweiler!"

"It's yoghurt, icy water, sugar — or you can have it salty. Hey, I've been forgetting you're Daniel's sister. But just then, your expression was just like his. You're prettier though, by far!"

The drink was cool, sweet, soothing, fragrant. "Take me with you to see Daniel," I said. (Or take me *anywhere*, I thought.)

"What about your parents?" His eyes sharpened with reality.

"I don't care. I want to see Daniel. I want to see India. I want to flow with the current!"

"Hey Hannah, your Dad would kill me."

"See! You hold out some shiny possibility, talk about flowing with the current, then you get all stuffy and responsible."

"I guess I have a responsible side too. Let me think about it. How about dessert?"

We both ordered gulab jamun — fluffy ground-rice balls like golden islands in a pond of syrup.

"Don't you think Daniel wants to see me?" I asked, not so easily distracted from the idea of the trip which was becoming more magnetic by the minute.

"I know he really wants to see you. It's been a tough time for him. And sometimes India seems like a long way from home."

"So, take me. I'm not a child."

"I'm aware of that; *very* aware of it."

There was a new power in me. I knew he couldn't easily say no. When he held my eyes it was at least in part because mine were holding his. The feeling was like sunrise in my blood.

"Let me come, Casey. Show me India on the way. You know you want to."

"We might not be able to get you a place on the train. Usually you have to book in advance."

"So we could go by bus."

"I wouldn't recommend it."

"I know we can get there somehow."

He smiled in defeat. "You're not going to give up, are you? We'll have to leave early. You will be sure to leave a note telling your parents you'll be back on Thursday."

"That's only four days. It wouldn't be worth it for less than a week. And it'll give them a holiday too."

"Are you sure?"

"More sure than I've ever been about anything."

"I'll have to pick you up from your hotel at five tomorrow morning."

"Five?"

"The train goes early. And we need to allow extra time to sort out a ticket for you. Are you sure you want to do this?"

"Even if it was three in the morning!"

"I'd better walk you back as soon as we've finished. You'll need an early night."

Familiar Hannah Jarvis had disappeared. Someone new had stepped out of the mirror. Ah, night as sweet as gulab jamun!

EIGHTEEN

But sweetness is a fleeting trick of the tongue.

When I got back to the hotel, Mum was sitting on the worn leather sofa in the reception area reading the massive paperback she'd started on the flight.

"Dad wants us to join him. He's having a drink in the courtyard."

"Am I in trouble for going out?"

"No. He hardly noticed. He's really upset about Daniel, I think."

The hotel restaurant has some tables outside and Dad was drinking Kingfisher Beer. His face looked flushed and flabbier than usual — as if the muscles had all gone slack.

A frequent zap came from the blue neon mosquito fryer.

Mum and I took our seats and ordered soft drinks.

"I'm going to the Embassy in the morning," Dad announced. "I'll tell them Daniel's here and ask for their help to find him and get him home."

"You can't," Mum pleaded. "He'll end up in prison. He'll phone in a day or two when Casey's talked to him."

"Prison might make a man of him. He can't run away for ever."

"And what if he's innocent?" I asked.

"Innocent?" The word seemed to burn Dad's mouth.

"Mum's right. We should give it a few more days before we do anything. You haven't enjoyed your holiday yet. You've escaped from work, now's the time to relax and do some sightseeing."

"I'm not familiar with relaxation. Never have been. And there's no chance now." Were Dad's words slightly slurred? Or was it just that he was talking quietly so as not to draw attention to us. Not that there were any other guests around to notice — only the waiter who was probably taking a nap in the kitchen now he had served us.

Another mosquito fried in a flash of blue.

"Give it just a few more days. Go easy on him." Mum put a hand on Dad's arm.

"Go easy on him! If I hadn't always followed your advice to go easy on him, he might be a different person now." Dad shook her hand off. It was the familiar argument but threateningly unfamiliar to hear it clawing the Indian night.

"If you just showed him you cared instead of always trying to change him, you might get somewhere." Their voices were almost breaking with barely constrained frustration.

"Spare me the psychology! How about him showing us he cares? I mean, how selfish can you get? First he says he'll meet us here, then he just doesn't show up."

"He's scared."

"My point exactly. The boy has no guts. Ross was never like this."

"Some parents were arranging kidnaps, Dad. Jody told me about it." I hate it when Dad runs Daniel down. I had to say something.

Dad turned to me, ready to fight any opponent, but softened a little.

"You really don't understand this, Hannah. Daniel has let us all down. What sort of person sends his friend to make excuses when his parents have travelled from Australia to see him? That Casey must have rocks in his head to do Daniel's dirty work."

"It was so generous of him to come," Mum leapt in. "I think he's a real friend to Daniel."

"God, you make me sick! You make excuses for every lame dog. We'd better finish this in private. Go to bed, Hannah. You don't need to hear this."

"But ..."

"Just go!" Dad thumped his beer bottle down to emphasise his words. It was no time to stick around.

When I turned back at the courtyard entrance, they had forgotten me and resumed their argument, stabbing at each other viciously with impatient gestures and words designed to wound.

Two mosquitoes in quick succession flew into the beguiling blue of death. The garden was full of shadows; long, pointed leaves and night-muted greens.

The noise of the streets kept me awake. And wondering if I should really go with Casey. The simple certainty of earlier in the evening had been a butterfly, now dashed to the ground. Hot night curled around me like tentacles and thoughts writhed around in my mind. Did Mum need me to be here? Could I trust Casey? Should I give up on seeing Daniel? But wouldn't seeing him make the whole trip worthwhile for all of us? What if Dad sent the police after us? Somewhere in the night a woman wailed. I was aware again that this country was a stranger. The thought of going terrified me. The thought of not going and losing the only chance to see Daniel was like a lead blanket. Either way, I would have to be up before five either to go with Casey or to tell him I wasn't going. I wasn't sure which it would be when I checked I'd set the alarm properly and finally drifted into the sweat-damp sheets.

Sharp sound in darkness. Cool shower over blurry eyes. Clothes and camera packed. Is she going? Pen writes note. All so simple really.

Man waits; a grey shadow by a white pillar in still-dark morning. She senses the warmth of his body. Golden hair uncombed, eyes still soft with sleep. He whispers, "Are you ready? Everything okay?"

"Yes. Let's go." Nervous whispered laugh she hardly recognises as her own.

He puts a strong arm around her and walks her away from all she knows.

NINETEEN

The sun rose over a misty raspberry river. Women swayed down towards a small temple on the banks, brass water-carriers on their heads, laughter in their movements. The train rumbled across the wooden bridge, carriages shining pink and gold. I smiled and smiled again.

The bustle of Bombay, the station platform with enough people to fill a football stadium, all that was left behind. Not that the landscape was ever empty. Figures moved from here to there beside the tracks, on bicycles or leading water buffalo, carrying provisions to villages, or herding animals. Some stopped to stare at the train, clusters of brown eyes giving nothing away. Inside our first-class carriage, a girl in a spotless turquoise frock and patent shoes looked out at other children, barefoot and ragged, running along beside the train, shouting and waving. Our carriage princess remained passive, unmoving.

"First class?" I'd said to Casey. "Are you rich or something?"

"Foreigners usually travel first or second class. It's not expensive by our standards. I tried third class for the experience, but I wouldn't recommend it unless you want to be packed like cattle, along with the chooks and goats of course.

There's air-conditioned first class too, but it's icy and isolated behind the closed windows."

Now we sat in quiet splendour, our only companions an Indian family, regal and polite. Banks of electric fans cooled us, circulating dust as well as air.

We didn't say much. Warmth, the effects of a restless night and the regular motion lulled me into semi-sleep. Then we stopped at a station somewhere and all was noise and activity again. Guys holding trays above the crowds came to the train windows with chai and sweets, bananas and magazines, fried snacks and slices of coconut, bottles of soft drink and trinkets for children. People shouted and threw "luggage" tied in bundles of cloth or passed suitcases over heads. How could more people possibly fit in the carriages that were already bulging with passengers hanging out of windows to get some space? Perhaps this was the last train to paradise?

Casey smiled at me, amused I think at my aghast expression. "You'll get used to it," he whispered. "Do you want anything to eat or drink?"

I shook my head. We'd bought snacks and bottled juice before boarding in Bombay. Spicy fried samosas for breakfast had been a shock to my system and my stomach was gurgling ominously.

Eventually the train lurched off again leaving crowds in its wake.

"You'll like it at Mahaban," Casey said. "It's cooler than down on the plains and the views are fantastic."

"It seems to get hotter every day."

"The next couple of months are stifling, they say. Then the monsoon comes and brings some relief. Still glad you came?"

"This journey is amazing. But I'm a bit worried about Mum and Dad. I mean, what if they send the police after us or something?"

"They wouldn't do that, would they?" Casey rubbed his eyebrow thoughtfully.

"No, I don't think so. They've got enough to sort out with their own lives." I wasn't as sure as I sounded and Casey's expression told me he had taken my words seriously.

He grasped my arm. "If you've set this up to lead them to Daniel, Hannah, you're doing the wrong thing. Tell me now and I can still take you back." The confident voice had taken on a fierceness I couldn't have imagined a few minutes before.

"How could you think that! You suggested it in the first place." I moved away from him and looked out of the window, realising I was travelling with a stranger.

"Okay." Then after a moment, "Sorry, Hannah. I'm just worried about this. Worried about Daniel and doing the best for him, worried about you and whether I should be doing this at all." He moved closer, speaking quietly, lips close to my ear so the other passengers wouldn't hear. He took my arm again, this time with soothing persuasion.

I felt like a river that has found the ocean — scared of being swallowed up but unable to resist the long-awaited delight of surrender. I realised guiltily that I was caring less and less about seeing Daniel. Only the journey with Casey mattered.

The little station where we changed trains was heat-paralysed. People moved in slow motion and sounds were muffled in the dense air. When the Bombay train continued on its journey, even the hawkers retreated to a cooler spot, leaving us almost alone. We crossed to another platform for the special narrow-gauge railway to Mahaban. Everything shimmered, mirage like, and we sat on a bench in the narrow band of shade outside the "Ladies Waiting Room". The hills rose steep and dry to a cloudless sky.

"It feels like a dream," I murmured to Casey.

"And Australia is reality?"

"No. That's a dream from many months ago. At least this is today's dream."

The silence of intense heat was a weight paralysing all thoughts and movement. We were sitting close enough that his hand, relaxed on the bench, was just touching my leg. It was too casual to be deliberate but surely too close to be accidental. He gazed out to the mountains, as if totally unaware of creating heat within heat, dreams within a dream.

Maybe minutes. Maybe hours. Maybe no time at all. Slightest hot breeze caresses sandalled feet. Tears of perspiration trickle warm and unhurried. Damp sheen pastes tendrils of man's fair hair to freckled forehead. Young woman waits.

Train arrives, slow, noisy, steaming. People emerge from nowhere and everywhere. Man takes young woman's hand and leads her further from familiarity. Bodies push close on packed seats. Damp shoulder to damp shoulder, warm leg against warm leg. Smells of foreign sweat and hot hills. Rhythmic sounds of train on tracks. Eyes watching, faces shining, heat enveloping all. Nothing to say. Nothing to say. Only feel. And live. And live.

The plains recede. The train slowly consumes steep slopes of dust and bush. Summit beckons holidaymakers and hopefuls to its cooler, shaded air. From here to there in a languid hour.

Back on solid platform, people shout and call again. Heat retreats back down the massive twisted hillside.

Casey takes my hand again. "Well, this is it," he says.

We stopped for a cool drink in a shady café on the red-dirt main street before hailing a scooter-taxi to take as out to the "hotel" where Daniel was staying.

"Do you think he'll be pleased to see me?" I asked Casey as we bumped along the pot-holed road.

"Of course!"

"It's so long since I've seen him. I can't believe I've come all this way." The warm, dusty breeze came through the open sides of the "taxi" covering the bags between our feet with a fine film of red. I wriggled the stiffness out of my shoulders and smiled.

"You look like a real adventurer!" Casey said. "Quite a different woman from the one sipping drinks in a fine Bombay hotel."

"Does that mean I look a mess?"

"Beautifully travel-ravaged," he said, reaching towards me and brushing a strand of hair away from my sticky forehead. "Crushed clothes and red dust become you!"

"I'd better get showered and changed before we see Daniel."

"Whatever you want. But there are some things you can't wash away."

His cryptic comment was left without response as the taxi scrunched to a halt outside a sprawling wooden building called "Mountain Lodge: Cheap Rooms".

In the dim, fan-cooled reception area a young Indian guy with a chubby face was putting mail in cubbyholes behind the long mahogany desk.

"I'm sharing with Daniel Jarvis, Room 18. My friend here needs a single room. Do you have any close to Room 18?" Casey asked.

"Friend in Room 18 is leaving yesterday," the guy said with a slight bow of his head. "Room 18 still free if you want."

"Left? Where? Did he say where he was going?"

"He is leaving a note. Your name is?"

"Casey. Casey Phipps."

The receptionist looked through a few envelopes in an unnumbered cubbyhole. "Yes, for you Mr Phipps, he is leaving a letter." He handed Casey an envelope.

Casey read it without showing me. "Well, he hasn't gone far," he said, looking relieved. "But it's probably best if we stay here. He's moved in with some others from The Tribe who have shown up. I don't know the place they're staying. It's a private house down the other end of the plateau somewhere."

"We'll stay two nights," Casey told the receptionist.

"One room?" the receptionist asked.

Did Casey hesitate a fraction of a second before answering?

"No. Two rooms. Two rooms near each other. You have rooms with private bathroom?"

"One left only."

"Give that one to my friend here. You have a room close to the room with bathroom?"

"Attached. Side by side."

"Good."

We took our keys and walked down the shaded path. All the rooms were on ground level and had a veranda and shuttered windows overlooking the path and garden. Ours were in a separate extension at the very end of the track, looking out across a sun-scorched lawn to tall trees.

"What now?" I asked.

"A shower. Then see how we feel. We could go and find Daniel today, but it might be better to leave it until the morning."

We opened our doors and went into the adjacent rooms.

I dropped my bag on the floor and tested the bed. Not springy, but covered with clean white sheets and a grey blanket. The bathroom was white-tiled and smelt of pine cleaner. I slid the wardrobe door open and noted the four coat-hangers. Lucky I wasn't planning on dressing up. There was another door. I turned the dull stainless steel knob and walked through. There was Casey, stripped to the waist, delving in his bag.

"Oh sorry!" I said. "I didn't know."

He looked up, surprised, and then laughed. "They must let these two out to families as a suite. Shall I see if they've got a key to lock it?"

"No need," I said. "I won't barge in again."

"I like it that you trust me," he said.

Did I trust him? Did I trust myself? Was it anything to do with trust? Not really. It was just that uncertainty and un-known possibility seemed to suit the new me better than the security of a locked door.

"Who were the other people Daniel went off with?" I asked Casey as we ate dinner in the Lodge's restaurant. There were few diners in a vast room which probably hadn't changed for fifty years. Once it would have been very elegant with its wood panelling, white tablecloths, silver cutlery and polished floor. Now it seemed slightly sad, with slowly rumbling ceiling fans, slow service from elderly waiters, and chips in the white plates that had "Mountain Lodge" in maroon script, scratched and scraped from endless washing up.

"A guy called Troy, who was a friend of Daniel's — and a couple of others — he didn't say who."

"I think I met Troy. He had a ute and picked Daniel up when he left home."

"That'd be him. One of the early members of The Tribe. He was a sort of "right-hand man" to The Poet. Lennox was in a similar position but Troy had been around longer. He was studying law but gave it up to take care of the administrative stuff at Miralee. If he's here, it could mean there's news from The Poet."

"I still don't understand all you guys — and girls — following The Poet. Can't you just get on with your ordinary lives and still listen to what he says?"

"It's not that simple. It's not just like information you can pick up from a book. We're talking about a whole different way of life which is much easier with a living example and others who want to do the same thing. Don't you ever wonder why you're alive? How you're meant to live?"

"Sure, it's crossed my mind, but you could search all your life and never know the answer to that."

"But what if, by searching, you *could* find the answer to those questions? People like The Poet say that by a long process of spiritual work the Truth is revealed more and more."

"Sounds risky to me. What if you spend years doing all that for nothing when you could have been enjoying your life?"

"I'm enjoying my life this way. Who says I'd be enjoying it more if I was working forty hours a week, trying to meet the house and car repayments, going out getting drunk on the weekend?"

"But what if you get to forty or fifty and you still don't have the answers you're looking for? Won't you regret all that wasted time?"

"You don't waste any time if you're really present NOW. Other people waste time by trying to build up things for the future. The key to all this is to be here now, this minute."

"I'm always here now, this minute."

"Not if your thoughts and dreams are elsewhere."

"Talking of thoughts elsewhere. I can't wait to see Daniel now we're so close."

"First thing after breakfast tomorrow we'll go. In the meantime, don't miss this moment."

His hand reaches for hers across the table. Eyes lock and hold her in vulnerability. Clangs from the kitchen and the rumbling fan stir the air but not the space they sit in. She looks away and removes her hand to take a fork again but not before recognition has passed between them.

Palest yellow voile of almost-full moon. Rich silk of jasmine fragrance. She wraps herself in a cloak of the night but knows she's naked to him anyway. At the doorway he kisses her, filling her body with warmth and knowledge. Just one kiss. Too long for mere friendship, too short to fill the yearning of years.

She listens to sounds of him moving around in the next room. Imagines his body draped in the sheets of cool cotton. Then closes out the invading thoughts that creep through the shadows, and tries to pull down the blind of sleep.

TWENTY

The motor rickshaw driver swerved expertly to avoid the worst of the potholes in the dirt road. The sun was already warm and Casey was smiling.

"You've come a long way for this," he said.

I nodded. Had a kiss changed anything between us? Casey was acting no differently towards me this morning. "I won't know what to say to him when we get there."

"Of course you will. He won't have changed that much."

Mahaban was peaceful after Bombay. People walked along the dirt roads but the movement was slower, the air cleaner apart from the small clouds of red dust disturbed by the occasional vehicle.

Away from the small town, the road lost a little height and went through bushland and trees. Almost at the rim of the plateau a short fork from the main road ended at a formal gateway with brick posts. A fair-haired guy in baggy Indian pants was sitting on a wooden chair watching us. Casey paid the driver and went over to him.

"We've come to see a friend, Daniel Jarvis," he said.

"Sorry, I can't let anyone in. There's an important meeting going on today."

"Hey, I was at Miralee. Can we wait around and see Daniel when the meeting's finished?"

"I can't let anyone in at the moment." Then he spoke into his walkie-talkie. "Lena, it's Matt. There are a couple of people here who want to visit Daniel. The guy says he was at Miralee."

Casey's smile had evaporated. He paced about in front of the gate while I waited in a spot of shadow beside the opposite gatepost to the gatekeeper.

"Lena's coming down to see you in a minute," the guard informed us.

A woman in a silky blue pantsuit appeared about ten minutes later and unlocked the padlock which held massive chains around the gate.

She smiled when she saw Casey and pushed her thick dark hair back from her face. "Hi, Casey, good to see you." She hugged him. "It's wonderful you're here. I think there will be some good news after today's meeting." I was feeling awkward, waiting for their long-lost-friends-number to finish. "Who's this?" the woman asked Casey with a non-committal glance in my direction.

"This is my friend Hannah, Daniel's sister. She's come all the way from Oz to visit him."

"Oh. It's just Tribe members today. There aren't any facilities for visitors here — it's just a temporary rental."

"She doesn't need facilities. She's just here to say hi to Daniel. It's just, you know, a family visit."

"We're having a meeting about a new development in the Tribe's direction. It's about to start now if you want to join us. Your friend can come back in an hour or so."

"If Hannah can't come in, I'm not coming in. We'll be back in an hour."

"What shall we do now?" I asked, once we were out of Lena's hearing range.

"Let's see if we can find somewhere to look at the view. If there's a lookout on this edge, it should be spectacular."

Casey didn't say anything while we sweated up the hill to the main track. When I lagged behind, he took my hand to pull me for a while. From there we followed the road around the ridge for about half a kilometre. "Do you think I'll ever get to see Daniel?" I asked, sighing as much from the heat and exertion as from a growing sense of pessimism.

"Ssh. We'll talk in a minute. Save your energy. We won't go much further unless we find a track to the edge. I've got a bottle of water in my bag but not enough for a major walk in the heat."

It was more like ten minutes before we saw a weathered sign saying "Best West Lookout and Café".

"Thank God," I said.

"Thank Its-Supreme-Mysteriousness, you mean."

The café was a wooden kiosk with a couple of benches just within the strip of shade where the trees ended. The "manager", who looked no more than twelve, found us both a nameless orange soft drink from an esky full of water.

There was still an expanse of rock and scrub between us and the mountain edge, but you could sense the massive bowl of air from our almost-rimside seat. The fizzy orange drink was cool to the mouth but acidy sweet, coating teeth in a sticky residue.

"It never used to be like that at Miralee," Casey said, wiping bright orange from his mouth to the back of his hand. "Guards and rules, I mean."

"I guess they're all a bit jumpy after the shooting. What if they don't let me see Daniel?"

"Of course they'll let you see him. We just picked the wrong moment, that's all. Come on, let's look at the view. You're not scared of heights are you?"

Below her, birds glide on thermals, dipping and swooping towards the dusty brown plains, deep in the ocean of space. On the far, far distant horizon are more high hills, hazy and bare. Though insignificant she is not diminished but stretched from earth to sky. Silence and space steal her boundaries. Minutes pass but nothing stirs her.

She turns and his eyes are as old as the land. He seems to speak but she hears no words, only feels the simultaneous touch of coolness and warmth, breeze and sun. His arm comes lightly round her shoulders and they turn away from the depths and the height, the far and the wide. "We must come back at sunset," he whispers. "And bring your wings."

We walked slowly back, sharing the warm water in Casey's bottle to wash away the sweetness from the sticky caverns of our mouths.

The guard started speaking into his walkie-talkie as soon as he saw us approaching. "Daniel won't be long," he said. "Hot, eh?"

We nodded and retreated to a meagre patch of shade.

"Do I look okay?" I asked Casey, aware that I probably looked like I do after sport.

"Beautiful."

Then, within minutes, chains clanked as the gate was unlocked and there was Daniel.

TWENTY-ONE

We stared at each other for seconds. He looked thinner and softer somehow.

"Hey guys, great to see you!" he said. "I've missed you heaps, Hannah." He hugged me longer and harder than he would have done at home and put an arm round Casey in greeting. "Let's go into town for lunch. I've only got a couple of hours. There are usually a few rickshaws waiting for business back up the road a bit, by the cemetery."

"Hasn't anyone told them those folks are dead?" Casey said.

"It's the earth and maggots they leave in the rickshaw that are the problem," Daniel replied, but as soon as the laughter faded, so did the openness in his eyes. "How are Mum and Dad?" he asked me.

"Good. Well, maybe not so good. There was an argument before I left to come up here. But they're well."

"I guess they weren't too happy I wouldn't see them."

"Of course they weren't. It's a long way to come for someone who doesn't want to see you."

"In a way, I *would* like to see them. But everything's too much of a mess at the moment. And you never know with

Dad. He'd rather use force than admit defeat. Has Casey been looking after you?"

"She doesn't need 'looking after'," Casey replied before I could. "But we've been sticking together."

"Not too close, I hope. Casey's got a reputation with the women, you know."

"Take no notice," Casey said. "My reputation has no basis in reality."

"No smoke without fire. And a fire crew would need breathing apparatus around you."

"Your brother, on the other hand, has decided to join a monastery and dispense with women in his life. Talking of monasteries, what's the story with all this security and secrecy, Dan?"

"Everyone's nervous since the shooting. And you know what Lena's like; she's inclined to get into her power number. Hey, it's great you came today. I've decided to move on from here in a couple of days. I was really hoping you'd make it before I leave, Hannah."

"What's the rush to move?" asked Casey. "Hannah will be here for five days. And I've promised to take her back before I can go anywhere else."

"I just don't feel so comfortable hanging out with the Tribe since the shooting. Not everyone thinks The Poet's instruction of being non-judgmental and forgiving should apply in my case. You don't have to come with me, Casey. We could meet up again in a couple of weeks."

We found a rickshaw driver dozing in his rickshaw beneath a banyan tree and rode back into town. In a first-floor restaurant where we could watch the movement in the red-dirt street through tatty flyscreens, we ordered thalis and dunked Nan bread in the little stainless steel bowls of spicy curries.

I kept looking at the two guys. Daniel seemed older than I remembered him, but there was also a calmer quality about him. And I looked at Casey afresh too, watching him talk to

Daniel, noticing the way his hair curled and the softness of his travel-worn T-shirt, not-quite-white against his gold-dust skin.

There was so much I wanted to ask, but it seemed a bit too blunt to blurt it out without steering the conversation gently in the right direction first.

"What was the meeting about?" Casey asked.

"Strange things. Apparently Melissa has got a message from The Poet, and Lennox is coming to talk to us all about it."

"Fantastic! Where is he? The Poet I mean."

"I don't know. Lena just got an e-mail from Lennox with his flight details. I don't think Melissa's coming."

Casey was watching Daniel's expression closely, the psychologist reading the signs. "You're not keen on those two, are you?"

"Melissa's okay."

"Are you sure you don't want to stay and hear what it's all about?"

"I'll phone in a few days. If The Poet's coming here, I won't be that far away. Hell, if anyone had told me a year ago that I'd be in India evading an attempted murder charge and discussing a guru, I'd have thought they were out of their tree."

I put my fork down, mouth burning after a piece of lime pickle. "What are you going to do, Daniel? When the money runs out, I mean. You can't stay in India forever."

"I know. I'll have to come back and give myself up. I've been thinking a lot about it. I can't live a life in hiding. Better to get it over with."

"But you didn't do it. Just tell them you didn't do it!"

"Do you believe I didn't do it?"

"If you say you didn't, I believe you."

"I wish everyone saw it that simply." He looked down and scratched at a mark on the stainless steel tray.

"But you didn't do it." Casey joined in the conversation now. "And you know who did, don't you?"

"Don't even ask me. It might be better for me to take the rap. Is there any news of Jessica?"

I looked at Casey questioningly as if he might be able to shed light on the situation, but he looked bewildered too.

"We'll have to talk about this some more, Dan. I know you're fed up with me saying it, but you just have to tell the police the truth." Casey spoke softly but insistently.

"I don't want to talk about it. There's nothing more to say. End of story. Is there any news of Jessica?"

"The police haven't told us anything and the TV teams seem to have forgotten you for a while at least." Then I added, in almost a whisper, "No doubt we'd hear if she got better — or worse. I just can't believe you'd do something like that. You didn't, did you?"

"Just drop it," he said. "I'll look after my own life. The best thing you can do for me is not keep hassling me. Don't spoil this time. Please let's just enjoy ourselves."

Casey reached out and held my hand under the table, both as reassurance and a warning to leave it alone, I think. But, after that, we all seemed to step awkwardly around the subject as if it were a heap of shit just waiting to be trodden in.

"Just going over to the shop," Casey said. "I'll give you two a bit of 'family time'."

Daniel looked at me almost shyly. "Are you liking India?" he asked.

"I just love it. I can't imagine being back at school after all this."

"It's another world, eh? You get to miss things though when you've been here awhile."

"Like what?"

"Good chocolate. Mum's salads — though I'd never have believed it. Proper TV. Space without people. Vegemite of course. And nagging younger sisters! Have you spoken to Jody recently?"

"Yeah, I have some things from her for you but they're back at the Lodge. We could go back up there and get them if you like. Or I can bring them tomorrow. I took some photos of her too."

"Perhaps we should get them now. I was going to do some work tomorrow — be a bit useful before I disappear — there are loads of renovations going on."

"I can visit you, can't I? It can be in the evening if you're busy in the day."

"I hope so. Officially it's 'no outside visitors' at the moment, but I'll ask Lena. This is just a difficult week with all the changes."

"Just my luck to have picked the wrong moment after coming halfway round the world."

"Its-Supreme-Mysteriousness works in strange ways. But it's great seeing you, Hannah. I'm heaps glad you came."

"Will you phone Mum and Dad at the hotel? They really want to talk to you. And they might not freak out so much about me being here if you tell them I'm okay."

"I guess I should. But I just couldn't stand a lecture right now."

"I can't guarantee Dad. But Mum won't give you a hard time."

"I'll try tonight."

Within another half hour, I'd given him the packages from Jody, and he'd disappeared again in a puff of rickshaw smoke.

Casey and I had tea served on his balcony. "What do you think?" I asked. "About Daniel. That bit about the shooting was weird. And he seems so flat. Though he used to be scary when he was fighting everything, I think I preferred it to this defeated acceptance of something so unfair."

"Something's going on he doesn't want to talk about. He

does seem depressed at times. I wondered if he'd tell you more when you were alone."

"No. He'd be more likely to talk to you, I think. Will you go and spend time at the house with him?"

"I was thinking I should go down tomorrow and see what's happening. Would you be okay on your own for the day?"

"Sure. But I want to see some more of Daniel. Its-Supreme-Mysteriousness has got a lot of explaining to do as far as I'm concerned."

"I'm sure you'll be allowed to visit. I'll sort it out tomorrow." He drained the last of his chai. "Let's have a siesta and, if you're still up for it, we'll go and see that sunset."

It was easy to doze in the warmth of the afternoon and I needed a shower to wake me up again. My hair was still wet when Casey knocked on the door.

The streets were getting busier in the late afternoon and smells of spiced cooking were rich in the air. I was getting used to the bumpy, dusty rickshaws with their high-revving motor-scooter engines, fishy exhaust fumes and seats polished ultra-smooth by thousands of saris and polyester pants.

Once the rickshaw had beetled off into the maple light, with instructions to return in an hour, we walked along the gravelly path and were alone. The mountain edge seemed to be on the boundary of time as well as the closest point to heaven. The merest haze, saturated with a tangerine glow, turned the distance soft-focus. The far-off sound of a child's cry and a dog barking drifted up to us from somewhere in the deep cradle of humanity below.

They sit, just touching. Wordless. Waiting. Dissolved in the ocean of glowing colour. Without boundaries. Heavy and inevitable, the crimson sphere slips slowly on its journey of a thousand million years. Life seems to hang motionless. Then, slowly it releases the breath held in awe, as the last glow is extinguished behind the dark shadows of the hills. Cooler tones of twilight fill the vacuum and first stars become visible in the veiled dome. Stillness.

Impatient buzz of rickshaw tears at timeless fabric. He takes her hand and, still filled with silence, they walk back towards the road. She feels the warmth of their melded palms, the cool of night on her face. Lips come together and hold the heat of the vanished day.

They bounce through darkness and dust, through crazy colours and lights of town, not needing to speak, not daring to touch.

He leads her through the familiar gardens. She doesn't ask where they are going. If he tells her, she might have to refuse.

With an arm around her waist he unlocks the door to his room and guides her through almost-darkness to his bed. She feels both power and powerlessness, victory and surrender. Eyes become accustomed to darkness and garden lights reflect off ceiling creating luminescence around body outlines. Her hair spreads around her on the pillow and he traces the shape of her face with steady hand.

A knock on the door breaks the boundary of their private world. They both hold still, listening. Then he moves to answer it while she hurries through the connecting door. She stands in the darkness, suddenly feeling guilty, exposed.

"Hi Dan." Casey's greeting has a hint of question in it.

"Had to come and tell you that if you want to be involved tomorrow, be down there by 9 o'clock. I have to run now, the rickshaw's waiting, but I'll say hello to Hannah quickly first."

"She just popped into town. She'll be back soon."

"You reckon she's safe out on her own? I wanted to tell her I just spoke to Mum on the phone. I had a major job convincing her Hannah was safe here and they didn't need to come after her. They were planning to go to the police in the morning but I think I persuaded her not to. Of course she still has to convince Dad. If there's any chance they'll come after Hannah, there's even more reason for me to go soon. I can take Hannah back to Bombay with me. But in the meantime, keep an eye on her, Casey. I told Mum I'd look after her while she was here."

"Sure. I've looked after you, haven't I? Any more in your family need Casey's protection?"

"I'm serious. And are you coming tomorrow?"

"Yep, I'm intrigued."

"Okay, see you then."

After a few moments Casey called out, "You can come back now."

"You lied to him."

"You hid. It amounts to the same." He stood up and put an arm around me. "Shall we carry on where we left off?" he whispered.

"No. I think I'd better go."

"Shall we go for dinner?"

"No. I don't think I'm hungry. It's time I *did* go into town on my own and have a look around."

"Are you angry with me?"

"No."

"Are you still okay about me going tomorrow?"

She says yes, but she isn't sure. Then she hurries to get a rickshaw and lets the colours and lights of town absorb her attention until some calm has returned. She buys crispy samosas from a stall with roaring gas lamp and eats them in the street, wiping greasy lips on slightly sunburnt arm. Then she returns for an early night, restless and listening for him moving in the next room. Once or twice she almost gets up and knocks on his door but she doesn't. In the morning she hears him go and immediately starts yearning for his return.

I washed a few clothes in the bathroom sink, using hand soap, trying to compensate for the lack of a plug by wedging a sock in its place. I'd brought the socks with me thinking it might be cooler here in the hilly heights but I hadn't needed them. I hung the washing on the little veranda where slabs of sunlight and shade alternated in sharp contrast. Strange, mournful birdcalls outside reminded me how far I was from home and I started to like the feeling of being all alone in this exotic land. There was a strange new peace in having all my usual connections untied and being free to drift. Eventually I sat on the veranda and wrote a letter to Jody. Then, in the heat of the day, I wrote some more of the story of Daniel, realising for the first time it was also my story.

TWENTY-TWO

After Casey returned from his visit to The Tribe, we had dinner in town, sharing creamy korma and pilau rice, ours the only white faces in a busy restaurant of Indians on holiday.

"You've been given the all-clear for a visit tomorrow," Casey informed me.

"I'm highly honoured," I said.

"I know all the formality seems stupid. But it's been an uncertain time and everyone feels a bit defensive. The latest news of Melissa receiving a message, and Lennox about to arrive, has stirred things up even more."

"I thought you'd all be serene and at peace, awaiting the next move from Its-Supreme-Mysteriousness."

"Lime pickle? Or are you sharp enough already?" He gave me a half-smile. "Anyway, Dan says come down tomorrow. He's leaving the day after."

"Where will he go?"

"He's heading north. Time to see the Taj Mahal and then maybe on to Nepal. He'll have to go via Bombay so you can travel back with him if you like."

"Or?"

"Or you can stay another couple of days here with me and I'll take you back as agreed."

"I don't want to be in your way."

"You'd better go back with Dan then." He watched my reaction, teasing, giving me long enough to doubt for a minute. "You wouldn't be in my way. If you want to stay, I think we could make good use of the time." A conspiratorial smile, gently binding me to him.

"Perhaps Daniel will think it's strange."

"Then you'd better explain why."

"Is everything always so simple for you?"

" 'Simple' is my middle name." A pause while he sorts out a more considered answer. "I suppose I really don't like things confused and messy. Why complicate life more than it is already?"

"But you've got involved with Daniel and his situation is a mess."

"That, to me, is a simple case of sticking by a good mate."

"And taking his sister on a tour of India?"

"Mm. That is simply a case of having had my arm twisted by an irresistible woman."

"You *are* simple!"

If I wasn't already transparently hooked, my choice to stay another couple of days said it all. He took my hand across the table, looking serious again.

"I wish you could have met The Poet, Hannah. He was — is — really something special."

"If you say so. But he seems to have caused a lot of trouble."

"It's not he who caused the trouble. If everyone followed his teachings there would be a lot less trouble."

"But someone among his own followers was prepared to use a gun. It's not a very good recommendation."

"Lena would say he has let all this happen to teach us something."

"Do you agree with that?"

"Not exactly. But we can learn from everything that happens. Even in a spiritual commune people's greed or ignorance can get the better of them and overcome any seedlings of higher potential."

"That's a pessimistic view."

"I'd like you to prove me wrong."

"So you believe people are basically bad."

"Not bad. But totally self-centred. And too easily manipulated by the cynical, the power-hungry and the greedy."

"And you don't think The Poet was manipulating you?"

"It's one of the paradoxes that when someone comes along with something truly intelligent and revolutionary to say, most of the world is highly suspicious. They don't want to hear anyone who might shake them out of their comfortable routine and solidified selfish ideas. If Christ came along now, most of the Christians would run in the opposite direction. Or crucify him."

"Do you really think they would?"

"Of course. He was a revolutionary. He told people to leave their families and follow him — to put their spiritual life first. How many people would do that if it inconvenienced them or dragged them out of their comfort zone? More korma?" I shook my head and he scraped the last of it from the serving dish. "Sorry, I get carried away. But I'm sure you'd enjoy The Poet's talks or books. Come tomorrow and you'll see we're not all weirdos. But I warn you, you might get commandeered into the renovation work."

"I'm still a bit scared of the whole thing, but as long as you and Daniel are around, I suppose I won't feel too awkward."

"You'll be fine. But if we're going to be up early, we'd better get back soon. I'm tired after today. I'd like to do a short meditation and get an early night."

He takes her hand as they walk between the fringes of foliage towards their rooms. He kisses her at the door. A kiss that makes her body dissolve at the edges but ends with an unspoken "Not yet". Not yet. But soon.

She sits at the tiny table beneath a bare bulb and writes some more. She senses she's lost track of who she is here — just a week or two away from familiarity and now the clear boundaries she'd drawn to define herself have become seriously eroded. She knows she is only a few steps away from knocking on his door and begging to share the night. But the few steps she takes are towards her own bed and the safer world of dreams.

TWENTY-THREE

The next day started before dawn with an attack of the dreaded "Delhi Belly". I suppose I'd done well to go that long without it. For an hour or so I thought negative thoughts, wondered about staying in my room for the day, felt sorry for myself. Casey advised just a little curd (the Indian equivalent of yoghurt) for breakfast. He ordered boiled water and stirred in some sugar and salt.

"It tastes pretty foul but it'll do you good," he said. "You're not a real traveller until you've sat — or squatted — on the toilet, moaning, wishing you were in your civilised bathroom at home! Take it easy and stay here today if you like. Are you sure it's not fear of the terrible Tribe that's making you sick?"

"Psychologists are hard to live with!" I muttered. "No, I'm *not* scared. I'll come along and see how it goes. I'm feeling better than I did."

But I was a little anxious, as well as strained in the stomach, when the rickshaw stopped outside the grand house. I'm not sure what I'd been expecting, but there was nothing particularly strange about the place. It could have been a colonial building in Australia with its wide verandas and cool interior.

Lena was sitting at a desk in the entrance area, and behind

her, stairs went up to a galleried first floor. Today, she was all smiles and welcomed me like a long-lost relative, getting up from her desk to hug both of us. "So glad you've come, Hannah. There aren't many of us here but maybe you'll get a little bit of the atmosphere of our Tribe. Just make yourself at home today. Back at Miralee we had a great library and facilities for visitors, but there's not so much to do here. The gardens at the back are great — you can sit in the gazebo and meditate. And Daniel will be pleased to see you, of course. If you're really bored and feel like giving us some help, Daniel is on the window-cleaning team today. We're tidying the place up in return for our temporary stay here. The owner of the place has great respect for The Poet — Indians are used to the concept of a guru and are so much more open to spiritual reality — and he spent some time at Miralee. How about you, Casey? Window cleaning or paint stripping upstairs?"

"I'll have a go at the paint stripping. It'll give Daniel and Hannah a bit of time together on the windows."

"Okay. Supplies are in the back room by the kitchen. Help yourself to disposable gloves too."

I wasn't sure I felt up to working, but there was really nothing else to do. I'd have been bored after five minutes meditating in the gazebo. We used pieces of Indian newspaper and vinegar to clean the windows. By the time I'd done the first one, my hands were black and I decided that the disposable gloves were a good option even though they trapped a layer of sweaty condensation in the heat. Daniel worked on the outside of a window while I did the inside, so there wasn't much opportunity for conversation. It was strange seeing him through glass, moving our arms in unison but never touching. Occasionally he made faces at me or stuck out his tongue, which suddenly made him my childhood brother again instead of the moody man I still hadn't quite got to know. From a portable CD player in the entrance hall, upbeat sitar music twisted an exotic melody through the high-ceilinged rooms. It was sweaty work but I found myself enjoying the physical activity and having a simple focus. The stomach cramps subsided. We worked clockwise around the house. In one room, a fragile-looking woman was washing the inside of a cupboard. She smiled and introduced herself as Tara but we didn't say much while we worked. Occasionally she hummed to herself in a tune that harmonised with the sitar music.

Late in the morning a gong sounded and Daniel mimed "lunch", pointed and shouted "back veranda". I wandered back into the entrance area, looking for somewhere to wash my hands. Lena was still holding the large gong-striker like the muscular man at the beginning of old movies. "There's a basin in the bathroom, first door on the left," she said when I held up my sweaty, grey palms. "You've been doing a great job."

As Daniel and I clambered onto the benches on either side of a long table on the back veranda, other people started appearing. In total, twelve of us sat down to lunch. Casey gave me a reassuring smile from the opposite end of the table, and when we were all seated, Lena said a sort of grace: "May we never take for granted this gift of life and may we use the energy from this food to increase our consciousness and bring peace to all".

Then Casey said, "Hey everyone, this is Hannah, Daniel's sister." He told me the names of everyone at the table and they all said "hi" and made a friendly or light-hearted comment, except Tara, who just smiled a regal acknowledgment. We passed around a large terracotta bowl of rice and a stainless steel pot of *mutter panir* — a spicy mixture of soft cheese squares and peas. In the middle of the table were heaps of bananas and some plates of coconut pieces. I took a small portion, not wanting to challenge my stomach too much.

A straggly-bearded guy next to me asked me where I was from and how long I'd be in India. Next to him, a Brazilian woman told me how she'd been visiting the Gold Coast while travelling around the world and had heard of The Poet from a friend there. She asked me how long I'd been in the Tribe.

"I'm just a visitor really," I explained.

"No one is *just* a visitor," she said. "We are all here for a reason, even if for a short time. Have you read The Poet's books?"

"No, not yet."

"Later, I will find one for you. There are three published. I know he will touch your heart. And you are the sister of this one?" She nodded towards Daniel. "He is a good worker. Very fine at many things."

At the other end of the table, Casey had an attentive audience as he described a scene in Bombay when a cow had been lying down in the street. "... And the whole street was blocked with rickshaws, bicycles and cars. A boy was trying to persuade this cow to move, pushing it and pulling it while the traffic backed up even further ..." He looked across at me and gave me a "haven't forgotten you" smile.

She watches them all watching him. How easily he plays to an audience. He glances in her direction. The look says she is his private audience, that she is holding the deeper part of him. She relaxes. Enjoys catching and throwing the ribbons of conversation that arc across the table. Warmth and laughter connect them all — a family whose members accept each other's idiosyncrasies with tolerant good humour. The Poet is occasionally mentioned — the absent patriarch, the invisible link between them. Casey pours cool water from the condensation-frosted jug. His eyes are searching for hers again and they don't let go easily. They are seeing each other anew; slight separateness bringing their closeness into fresh focus. Her smile unfolds. Barriers melt in the heat.

"When do you have to be back in Bombay?" Daniel asked me.

"Sunday. I'd thought of travelling back down with you but I'm enjoying the escape from parental tyranny! Would you mind if I don't come with you? Casey's happy to escort me back." The truth. Not the whole truth. Something like the truth.

"I'd feel bad about leaving you. I promised Mum I'd keep an eye on you. What's the big attraction here? Casey?"

"I really need some more time with him. Just a couple of days here. Please, Daniel, this is so important. I want it even more than I wanted to start school when you did."

"That much? It's always hard to say 'no' to you when you look so imploring. Shit, it's tough enough being responsible for myself without having to think what's best for you too. I'm in too much trouble already. Have you any idea how I'd feel if something bad happened to you and I wasn't here?"

"Nothing bad will happen. Casey's a 'responsible adult'. And in a traditional tribe, I'd be an adult too. I came here to see you, but suddenly just being here is the best thing that's ever happened in my life and I need a few more days to make the most of it — it's not the same sightseeing with Mum and Dad. Please, Daniel."

"I'll talk to Casey. I suppose I've trusted him this far."

"You're such an amazing brother!"

"Or a stupid one. I haven't said yes yet, okay?"

"Will you visit Mum and Dad in Bombay?"

"I've been thinking about that. In one way, I'd love to, but I can't face Dad at the moment. Best leave it until I'm back in Australia." He took another mouthful of lunch and changed the subject. "Will you see Jody when you get back to Queensland?"

"I promised to give her a first-hand report on you."

"You don't think she's forgotten me after all this time?"

"Not at all. You do still want to be with her, don't you?"

"Heaps. But so much has happened. I don't know if it'll be

the same when we see each other. She'd really be better to find someone less … someone with a simpler life."

"It's you she wants. I can't quite imagine how you two get on together, but she talks about you as if you're Mr Desirable himself."

"She's different from any other woman I've met. At first I found her sort of distracted and defensive, but when you get to know her, she's like being with half a dozen different women — gritty and tough one minute, your best friend the next minute, someone you want to protect an hour later. I keep getting drawn back to see what she'll be next." His enthusiasm broke through his cool for a moment. "But everything has got so complicated now. We don't really know each other. We just collided and some attraction held us together."

"Sounds good."

"It *was* good. You know, I thought I was getting my life right for once, but it didn't take me long to get in a fresh mess."

"It'll get sorted out for the best, I'm sure it will."

"Yeah, don't worry, Hannah. I'll find a way somehow."

When he turned away again to talk to someone else, I watched him, still looking for clues that would help me make sense of things. He looked so normal, toying with a banana skin and chatting to people. Yet as soon as he detached from a conversation, I saw him sink back into separateness.

By the end of the afternoon I was aching with a satisfied sort of tiredness. It was surprisingly good to be involved in the team spirit of the place. Other workers called out a greeting in passing as if I'd always been around. Paloma, the Brazilian woman, rushed up as Casey and I were about to leave. "Have this book," she said. "It is a spare copy. You need some payment for all your hard works! Do you have these leaflets?" She picked up a few leaflets from Lena's desk and tucked them inside the book.

"I hope you weren't too overwhelmed," Casey said, putting

an arm around me as we walked back up towards the cemetery rickshaw rank.

"I enjoyed it. But I'm not used to the hard work. My arms and legs are in shock. But at least my stomach has settled down."

"You don't have to come tomorrow. We can do something else if you like. Did you tell Daniel you were staying?"

"Yep. He's worried but getting used to the idea. I'd love to watch the sunset again but I couldn't stand to walk there today."

"I could carry you," he said, scooping me up. "Or perhaps we could make it a date for tomorrow."

"Tomorrow will be fine," I replied. "And I told Daniel we'd meet him for dinner at six."

A flock of green parrots took off from the banyan tree and a rickshaw driver looked at us disapprovingly.

"We shouldn't really be showing so much affection in public," Casey said. "Indians have different standards about these things."

As we set off in our bumpy, dusty carriage, I felt the first pang of having to leave, if not tomorrow then in a couple more days.

"Will you read it?" Casey asked, nodding towards the book Paloma had given me.

"I'll dip into it, at least. I guess I should try to understand what you folks see in the guy. Everyone seemed really friendly today."

"They're not a bad crowd. There's more optimism in the air again since the word of Lennox's arrival. Everyone's speculating whether The Poet will be setting up a longer term commune here."

"Would you stay in India then?"

"As long as I could. You have to leave to get a new visa every so often though. And the money won't last forever. I inherited a bit when Dad died but he wasn't rich. I could have saved it for a good down-payment on a house, but I feel about as settled as a nervous butterfly."

Lying under my cool white sheet later that evening, I opened The Poet's book. His words were plain but honest, a fabric of simple quality, like Indian silk in a shopful of day-glo synthetics. Chapter by chapter it was as if he was responding to questions I'd have asked if I'd thought anyone had the answers. He was talking to me. Not just to insignificant Hannah but to Hannah beyond time and place, Hannah beyond name and history.

She sits in the centre of a circle while her life events twirl around like frenzied dancers. Nothing touches her, though movement and colour shift into endless new patterns. Slowly she seems to dissolve into the air, looking down and seeing everything with the detachment of someone observing life from above. Problems are as insignificant as people passing on a distant road. The mountains and valleys of her life become part of one magnificent landscape.

Did I fall asleep for a moment? Calmness from the scene remained as I focused on the walls, readjusting to the solidity of semi-familiar surroundings. The sadness and worries about Daniel had totally dissolved. I knew I was ready to move forward, ready to make the most of every minute with Casey in the days we had left.

I closed the book and put it carefully beside the bed. For a few minutes I had tasted whatever it was that had attracted Daniel and Casey to The Poet. And I found myself looking forward to another day of work with the Tribe.

TWENTY-FOUR

The early morning shrouds India in softness. For less than an hour after dawn the familiar glare of heat is missing and even the incessant backdrop of noise is subdued. Casey gave me a wash-beaten *lunghi* to wrap around my shoulders like a shawl, and our rickshaw buzzed through the half-light, a thing of noisy purpose in the creeping colours which precede the sun. In town, a few shopkeepers were raising shutters, and other rickshaws joined ours in high-revving chorus. The first shafts of amber sunlight seeped along the platform as we arrived, awakening the small crowd of ghostlike figures to greater movement. Daniel was already there, wrapped up like a pale-skinned sherpa, with a massive backpack at his feet.

"There's something exciting about stations and airports," he said. "I'm really looking forward to seeing more of India."

"Don't you mind travelling alone?" I asked.

"There will be other travellers. You meet all the backpackers in the cheap accommodation places. And Casey's going to catch up with me again in a couple of weeks. I just want to make the most of my freedom before I have to go back to Australia and face the police."

"Take care. We want you back in one piece."

"Don't worry, I've had enough trouble for a while. I won't be trekking in disputed territories or studying the art of snake charming."

The minutes were visibly ticking away on the ancient station clock.

"And keep in touch. We want to know where you are."

"Poste Restante New Delhi is my next letter pick-up. And I'll be expecting a letter from both of you. Hey, I'd better get on this train or I won't be going anywhere. Give Mum a hug from me, Hannah, and say 'hi' to Dad. Tell Mum not to worry, though you might as well tell a fish not to swim."

"Bye Daniel. Come home soon."

He waved from the train as it started its downhill journey, leaving clusters of people like debris in its wake.

"We need breakfast," said Casey decisively, putting a firm arm around me and leading me away from the empty track.

There wasn't too much time to think about Daniel's departure before we were back in a rickshaw and off for another day's work with the Tribe.

The tall spaces of the old house were a refuge. I felt a different sense of belonging since reading some of The Poet's book. He had become a real person with a fresh vision to share, rather than some mysterious and rather threatening "leader". When people talked about him, I listened.

"There'll be no work tomorrow afternoon. Lennox is arriving off the morning train and there'll be a meeting at two o'clock," Lena announced at the end of the day. "Everyone is more than welcome to be at the meeting and hear the latest news of The Poet."

I wondered if she'd remembered me and that I wasn't a Tribe member, but I didn't ask if I was included.

"We'll have to put off our date with the sunset until tomorrow — we've left it too late to get there in time," Casey said looking skywards. "It's been a long day."

He was right. As our rickshaw bounced homewards, the

last light flared gold and it seemed as if a week had passed since the ebbing night had left pools of shadow in the same potholed tracks.

We stopped for an early evening meal and then strolled through the streets, fingers interlocked, not needing to say much. Later, we shared coffee on the veranda of my room, conversation drifting lazily between us. Our kisses were gentle, preludes to sleep.

"Are you sure you want to spend your last morning doing unpaid cleaning work?" Casey asked as he spread his toast with marmalade. Over the last four days these breakfasts had become our routine, but I never lost the sense of having slipped back in time. I imagined my mother would have had similar breakfasts during her English childhood. "We could look for souvenirs in town or just hang out together."

"At first I was only working to be with you and to see Daniel, but then I started to enjoy it. The last couple of days working together have been amazing. I never knew I could have so much fun with a dirty rag in my hand! Do you think I'll be allowed into the meeting this afternoon?"

"Just keep a low profile and come in with me. There are no big secrets. We'd better get going in a minute if you're determined to work."

"Will you stay in Bombay for a while when we get back there?" I was already looking for ways to prolong our time together.

"Just overnight. I can't travel both ways in one day and I need to see about booking a flight back."

"Perhaps you could come on the same flight as us."

"No. My return is to New Zealand with 'Cheap and Cheerful Airlines' — see ten Asian cities in the middle of the night tour!"

"When are you thinking of flying back?"

"It'll probably be another month or two. I'm not in a big

rush to get back but my money won't last for ever. I don't have any idea what I'm going to do or where I'm going to live when my gypsy life is over."

I wanted him to be in a big rush to see me. But it looked like at home Cinderella would turn back into a school student and there would be no travel dust between her toes. "Let's get going," I said. "We've got work to do."

Matt, the guard on the gate, just waved us through with a smile. Guitar music drifted through the open front door and was slowly absorbed into the warm air.

"Hi guys! What are you like at washing walls? I need six people for the old master bedroom which is going to be repainted." Lena had a clipboard and pen, which seemed a bit excessive for organising a dozen people.

"We'll do that," said Casey, looking to me for agreement as he volunteered us.

I nodded.

Mark (straggly beard) and Troy were among our work-mates. Mark had a portable stereo which pumped out music while we dipped our rags in warm water and wiped the pale peppermint walls. This majestic upstairs room looked out over the garden and gazebo to the edge of the mountain and distant sky.

We worked hard but it didn't stop anyone having fun. Jibes flew around, occasionally accompanied by a wrung-out rag or sponge.

I found myself smiling often. Not just because the guys were funny but because life seemed suddenly simple and good. I looked out and saw a hawk hovering high above the plains, rising and falling on the thermal currents. I looked at Casey and his eyes always seemed to penetrate to a part of me I hadn't even known before this week.

If my arms and legs hadn't been doubly aching, I wouldn't have even cared about stopping for lunch, but the sound of the gong was welcome and I was ravenous when the rice and vegetable curry hit my plate.

"You look like you're enjoying all this," Troy said, scooping up curry with a chapatti.

"I am. It's strange but I feel as if I belong here."

"That's exactly the feeling I've always had," he said.

I let the conversation and warm air wash around me. Mark offered to serve me more curry. "Banquet of Life, eh?" he smiled. "I was with the Hare Krishnas and the Children of Light before this, but I'm more at home here than anywhere."

"Lennox should be here anytime now," Lena informed us, and it was only five minutes later that the sound of a car outside sent her scurrying through the house, leaving her meal only half-eaten.

"Let's drink a toast to a whole new phase for the Tribe!" said Mark, raising his water glass.

"May we see The Poet again very soon," added Paloma clinking her glass against his. The rest of us raised our glasses and murmured some sort of agreement.

Lena never returned to her lunch and, by the time the pureed mango dessert arrived, conversations had restarted and were zigzagging in erratic patterns around the table. No one was in a rush to go anywhere and we sat another twenty minutes with our empty bowls. The last remnants of mango dried into sticky patterns and only a centimetre of water remained, now warm in the bottom of the jug.

Troy and Tara both checked their watches.

"Might as well start heading towards the meeting room," Troy said.

With washed hands and freshly combed hair we assembled in the grand lounge room. I stuck close to Casey and tried to look inconspicuous.

Our assorted chairs and cushions were in a semicircle around a large open fireplace partially concealed by an intricately embroidered peacock screen. A slightly squeaky fan cut heavily through the air, too high above our heads to move much of the sticky heat at ground level. A single chair faced all the others, waiting for Lennox.

Lennox looked elegant in a light beige suit which showed off his tan and brown eyes. For some reason everyone stood when he entered the room and he waved us back to our seats.

"Hi everyone. Isn't this a magnificent place? First, I want to thank you all for the work you've been doing here. I know The Poet would want me to acknowledge what a wonderful cooperative spirit has gone into the renovations. This is an excellent example of what we can achieve when we all work together. Its-Supreme-Mysteriousness has provided the perfect practice for our next task in bringing The Poet's words to a greater audience.

"As you have probably heard, Melissa is in communication with The Poet. This has given us fresh hope that he will return to teach us again before too long. He has instructed us to find suitable premises on the Gold Coast in Australia as a base for making the teachings accessible to more people. Miralee was perfect to provide solitude for our early days, but now we need somewhere the public can come for meditations and to discover this new way of living. Part of the good news is that Melissa and I have found an old warehouse by the river which is available at reasonable cost on a two-year lease. It will eventually be demolished to make way for road improvements but, with a few renovations, it will make a perfect base for us until then."

"What about the police?" asked Mark. "Won't they be giving us a hard time about the shooting?"

"Now they have the gun with Daniel's fingerprints, they shouldn't have any grounds to restrict the rest of us. They may want to ask us questions but we have nothing to hide."

"Where is The Poet now?" Troy asked.

"We don't know. Probably still doing his six-months silence somewhere in the Himalayas."

"I don't understand. How come he's talking to Melissa if he's in silence? Or is he writing?"

"The communication is at a deeper level. As some of you may know, Melissa is highly sensitive to vibration, and it was one evening when she was deep in meditation that she heard The Poet's voice speaking to her very clearly. At first she was unsure about revealing this to me — she thought I might not take her seriously. But, as any of you who have met Melissa know, she is a genuine spiritual seeker and is very sincere about doing The Poet's work. At first she doubted her own experience and said 'Why me?'. I thought about that and it became very clear why The Poet would have chosen her. First, she is someone sensitive enough to receive communication and someone highly trustworthy. Second, she is in partnership with me and, as you know, I have had a close relationship with The Poet since the early days. He knows that Melissa and I have the commitment and ability to continue making his vision a reality although he is not able to be with us now. I encouraged Melissa to write down what she hears whenever she receives a new message, and most days now there is some communication for us. Sometimes it might only be a few sentences; one day it was a whole page of teaching about trust." He looked around the room, fixing each of us with his laser eyes.

There was silence for a few seconds while everyone took in this new information. Faces didn't give much away and nobody seemed to want to be the first to respond. Eventually Mark asked, "How long has this been going on?"

"About two weeks. Last Saturday, Melissa received the message that we should build a new centre on the Gold Coast. You people are some of the key members of the Tribe and it seemed too important to just write or phone. The success of The Poet's new project depends on all of us working together with the same determination that you have demonstrated so wonderfully here. Melissa would have come too but she doesn't have a passport and we didn't want to waste time waiting for her to get the paperwork. The most important news of all is that The Poet has also told Melissa that when the centre is established, he will return and continue his work with us. I know we all want this more than anything and I'm sure you'll all be as keen as I am to start on the new place as soon as we possibly can."

One or two people clapped in agreement.

"Can we see the transcript of Melissa's messages?" Troy asked.

"I don't have them here but they will eventually be made available for further study."

"I can't see why The Poet wouldn't communicate in a normal way," Casey said.

"We have to trust he knows best," Lennox said, addressing the rest of us rather than Casey. "Before he left, he spoke about doing a retreat in the Himalayas — many of the great masters have spent periods in silence — and he never had a mobile phone!" There was a small ripple of laughter. "This is really a test for each of us and our trust in The Poet. Of course it is down to your own faith and commitment whether you participate in the new venture, but, personally, I will feel proud when he returns if I have helped create the new venue for his work."

"He always said 'faith' was for people who didn't have the commitment to find out the truth." Troy said.

"Perhaps 'trust' is a better word." He paused and addressed the rest of us. "Our friend Troy is always fast on his feet where The Poet's teaching is concerned. Thank you, Troy." His thanks had the smallest hint of sarcasm.

"The Poet always said he wasn't founding a religion and there was no room for priests in his organisation," Troy continued, undeterred.

"Your point being?" Lennox asked with the patience one shows an argumentative child.

"You and Melissa are becoming middle-men — sorry middle-people — between us and him."

"That's hardly the intention, Troy. We are simply messengers while he is unable to speak for himself. I think most of the Tribe are delighted that someone has been able to receive this guidance. Of course if you don't want to participate, no one is forcing you. The rest of us will be doing our best to continue his work."

"When will we be able to move into the warehouse?" Paloma asked.

"That's the right spirit!" Lennox said warmly and with a particularly appreciative smile. "My solicitor is reading over the lease while I'm away and, all being well, I should sign it when I get back. If you book your air tickets to return in a couple of weeks, you won't miss anything."

"What about money for the lease?" Casey asked.

"Well, I don't want to bore you with all the details now, but Rick Mulholland, Mal's son, has agreed to put up the advance money. As most of you already know, he is a Tribe member and let us use his home 'Miralee'. It's amazing how things unfold when you're working for the greater good."

"Legally you can't sign this on your own for The New Tribe." Troy said. "You need my signature and The Poet's, as agreed in our articles of association."

"As The Poet isn't around, I've decided to take it on in my name. It's the simplest way to get it all happening fast. With Rick as guarantor, there shouldn't be a problem." He sighed. "I really don't want to get bogged down in this sort of detail at the moment. Most of the Tribe members aren't interested in the legal technicalities. We mustn't lose sight of the bigger picture which is to get The Poet's work happening as fast as we can. Every day we delay might have been the day we could have made a difference to someone's life. Surely that's what matters most." One or two people nodded. "So let's commit ourselves wholeheartedly to making a difference in the world. To bringing the words of our beloved Poet to more people. I look forward to working with you all back in Australia. Thank you."

Lena stood up. "No more work this afternoon, folks. Take the rest of the day off. Those of you who think you would like to be involved back in Australia, come and see me at the reception desk at 4 pm and I'll put your names down."

Everyone was surprisingly quiet as we disassembled.

"What do you think?" Troy asked Casey back in the entrance hall. "Are you signing up?"

"Not this afternoon," said Casey. "This is Hannah's last day and we've got a date for the rest of the afternoon. How about you?"

"I'll talk to you later. Better not raise the voice of cynicism in these corridors!"

Casey caught up with Lena. "We're off to enjoy the afternoon. Hannah has to go back to Bombay tomorrow."

"Have a good trip back, Hannah. Thanks for all the work. I hope we'll see you on the Gold Coast. You live near there, don't you?"

"Yes, that's my home patch."

"You're not leaving us?" said Mark with exaggerated dismay, catching the tail of the conversation.

"I promised to be back in Bombay tomorrow," I explained.

"You mean you have better things to do than wipe eighty years of grime off slime-coloured walls!" Mark exclaimed. "And you're one of our best workers!"

"You'll manage without her," Casey assured him.

"But we'll miss you, Hannah," Mark said pleadingly.

"I wish I had a few more days here," I said.

"You must come and see us again in Australia," said Mark. "We promise to find equally dreary jobs for you!"

"Yes," added Paloma. "We hardly had time to get to know you."

Casey and I wandered around town, looking for little gifts

to buy. Everywhere was quiet in the afternoon heat, shopkeepers dozing in the back of their shops. When we'd exhausted the available treasure troves, and ourselves, we stopped for lime soda — soda water with oversized sharp bubbles poured over lime juice and sweetened with partially dissolved sugar. Nothing penetrates the crust of a dry mouth so well.

"What did you think of the meeting?" I asked.

"Mmm. Strange about Melissa and the messages. I was disappointed it wasn't something more concrete from The Poet. I know Melissa means well and I'm trying to keep an open mind but it's a bit hard to swallow the telepathic stuff."

"You think she might be making it up?"

"I don't think she'd deliberately make it up, but perhaps the borders between reality and imagination are a little blurred for her. I'm not totally closed to the possibility that people can get a feel for someone else's experience or thoughts by some inexplicable means though. Like when a mother knows her child is in danger. But this one is certainly stretching the boundaries of logic!"

"So will you come to the Gold Coast to help with the new centre?"

"I haven't had time to think it through yet. In one way, it may not be necessary to believe in the concrete reality of Melissa's guidance to take part in something which will help spread The Poet's teaching. Ask me again in a few days."

"I won't be here in a few days."

"You're right. Have you enjoyed your visit to Mahaban?"

"Too much. But I wish I could have done more to help Daniel while I was here."

"You've come a long way to see him. That counts big time. You can't do more than that. The rest is his responsibility."

"I suppose so. And it has been great for me here. I can't believe I ever thought of the Tribe as an evil cult. But I suppose people in evil cults don't think they're in evil cults either. How can you ever know for sure if you're just being conned? If you're being brainwashed into believing things?"

"That's a tough one. I'd believe my instincts, but some people have more reliable instincts than others. I guess you'd have to be suspicious if you're asked to do anything to harm yourself or anyone else. You can see how people could start to convince themselves that anything or anyone who gets in the way of their vision should be removed. That applies to business or politics as well as religion."

"Or love."

"Exactly. And the more the vision appeals to some inner hunger, the easier it is to put it before everything else. But 'the ends justify the means' always has to be a suspicious argument as far as I'm concerned. Come on, we've got time to shower and change before sunset. You don't want to miss your last hill station sunset, do you?"

"Don't keep reminding me that everything is the 'last'. It gives me a heavy feeling."

"Wisely said. Treat every experience as the first of its kind. The rest of your life is always beginning."

I washed the sweat of the day from my hair and body, noticing that my arms seemed to have become strong and supple in the few days here. I shook my head and tousled my fingers through my hair to help dry it. The long, ivory cheese-cloth dress that I'd bought in Bombay contrasted with my tanned skin and I hardly recognised the relaxed woman traveller that looked back from the scratched mirror.

"Wow," Casey said when he saw me. "From young woman to Goddess in under a week!"

He had changed into soft, clean clothes too, but the red dust quickly found its way back between our sandalled toes.

She sits, shoulder against his, feet dangling over the edge of the world. The moment is suspended in blazing tangerine and blast-furnace red. On the shadowed plain a few feeble curls of evening smoke rise like wraiths towards the primal fire. Hillside, hair and faces glow. A lone bird calls. The sun slips away. A wisp of pink cloud streaks the darkening sky. The warmth of earth is suddenly noticeable where it meets twilight coolness. He turns to kiss her and she breathes in the smell of India with the sweetness of his skin.

Tonight she is a woman. The woman. A million years of woman.

When he leads her back to his small bare room, where night scents of jasmine soften the air, she knows her transformation is complete. Bodies meld and melt. Words leave. Time slides under the door and heads for town. There is only the man and the woman.

TWENTY-FIVE

From there it was downhill of course. Downhill to the searing heat of the plains. Downhill from the height of life's experience to the dry riverbed of reality. It could have been totally depressing if I hadn't had Casey beside me to remind me that I was something more than I had been. There were still a few more hours of our joint journey to enjoy. It was a mixed feeling, an overlapping of the closeness we'd discovered in the last few days and the sadness of parting that was to come. Meanwhile, the flatlands of India unfolded outside the train window, passing in a plotless movie with a cast of thousands.

As the buildings became denser and we neared Bombay, I felt stretched — as if part of me was still in the hills and each kilometre of track was further straining my ability to be whole. I knew there was a limit to how far I could stretch before something would snap and a little bit of Hannah would be left behind. I wanted Casey to promise to come and be with me in Australia, but each time I formed the words inside my head they sounded mundane, corny somehow, compared with what we'd shared. To be honest, I was probably also scared of what his answer would be.

Bombay station seemed even more chaotic than when we'd left it. You would have thought it was Cup Final Day, except there were no signs of team colours. It was hard to move through the persistent lava flow of people seeping into every available space and crushing against each solid surface. My bag snagged against people I couldn't avoid, but Casey kept hold of my hand and forged ahead towards the exit.

Before we'd even reached the street, people were offering us taxis and hotels, grabbing to carry our bags or begging for money as we passed. It was a relief to scramble into the protective shell of a taxi.

"Don't look so sad," Casey said. "Or is it worry that's stolen your smile?"

"A bit of both perhaps. I feel like a runaway child about to face its angry parents."

"You *are* a runaway child."

"Thanks a lot. If I'm a child, you're a paedophile."

"I didn't mean it like that. Don't get touchy on me. You are their child. You will always be. And they're not used to you flying off from the nest on your own. Do you want me to come and see them with you? Or will your Dad lynch me?"

"I'd better test the water on my own first. What if they've left the hotel and gone on somewhere else?"

"I'll wait around in the taxi for ten minutes. If you don't come back, I'll know you've found them."

"Can we see each other this evening?"

"Of course. I don't want to miss our last evening together — sorry, delete the word 'last'. I'll be outside at six. And don't forget to smile!"

I went to the reception desk and asked if Mr and Mrs Jarvis were in their room.

"Mrs Jarvis said you are coming back today. We have a room for you. Number twenty-six." She handed me the key. "Mrs Jarvis is not in. She is returning at 4 pm."

"And Mr Jarvis?"

"He is leaving on business a few days ago."

I went to my room and opened the shutters which looked

into the courtyard garden. An old woman was bent over sweeping the terrace with a bundle of twigs that rasped against the stone. I kicked off my dusty sandals and lay down under the lallaping fan. Already I was missing Casey, my body aching for his touch, my eyes seeing emptiness where they should have seen him. The Poet's book was like a doorway back to a disappearing world. I opened it and let the words lead me. Slowly they took me from my small cell of sad emotions and showed me the place to stand for a clearer view.

But I didn't manage more than a couple of chapters before the words blurred together and the afternoon heat cocooned me in sleep.

The knock on the door came a couple of times before I dragged myself, sticky-eyed and tousle-haired, to answer it.

"Hi Mum." I smiled uncertainly, not sure whether to expect verbal abuse or a relieved reunion. Her pause showed me she wasn't sure which to dish up first.

"Were you asleep?" she asked.

"Yes. I got back a couple of hours ago."

"You look a mess. Are you okay?"

"Thanks! Yes, I'm fine."

"Don't think I'm happy about this."

"I know."

"I don't think you *do* know. I don't think you have any idea of the worry and problems you've caused."

"Mum —"

"I won't go on about it now but you're not let off the hook. Though I'm glad you're safely back. Let's have some tea in the garden. I want to hear all about Daniel. You did see him?" I nodded. "Good. Tidy yourself up and I'll see you downstairs in ten minutes."

"I *am* sorry, Mum. I didn't want you to be worried."

"Not as sorry as you should be. And how could I *not* be worried?"

The tea was served in a teapot with all the trimmings. It

seemed so natural now to be sitting in an Indian garden, sipping tea, thousands of kilometres from home.

"You look different," Mum said. "Are you really okay?"

"I'm fine. Don't fuss over me."

"Well I'm glad *you're* fine. I've been waiting here wondering whether I should follow you, not able to move from this hotel in case you came back."

"I told you I'd be gone for a week. And Daniel told you I was okay."

"But anything could have happened and I couldn't risk that you'd come back and find no one here."

"I hadn't thought of that."

"There doesn't seem to be anyone in this family who thinks further than what he or she wants to do. And I'm the idiot that has to try and compensate for everyone else's short-sightedness. Both you and your dad leaving like that is just too much."

"Where's Dad gone?"

"Perhaps you'll remember that he was upset even before you disappeared." Her tone was still cool, sarcastic. "Next day when he discovered you'd gone, it was the last straw. I thought he'd demand we follow you immediately, but he just got even more withdrawn. We eventually talked about it over dinner and decided to go to the police the next day. Then Daniel phoned and reassured me that you were okay, that he'd look after you. I asked him if he'd speak to Dad but he said, 'No, just say "hello" for me'."

"What did Dad say to that?"

"Naturally he was hurt that Daniel wouldn't speak to him. When I asked him what he thought we should do, he said there didn't seem to be much we could do. He said I'd spoilt you all and I could sort it out — if I had any bright ideas. He seemed more worried about you than Daniel at that point and said that if Daniel didn't look after you ... I can't remember what the threat was. Then he decided to go to Goa to have the holiday he'd come for. When I said we needed to stay here in case you came back early, he said I could wait if I wanted to; he was going."

"And you let him just walk off?"

"I said if we weren't going to operate as any sort of partnership, maybe we should reconsider our marriage."

"Well done."

"It didn't do any good. He left anyway. And I felt bad because I should have been more understanding with him."

"But you were right too."

"Maybe. There's going to be a lot to sort out when we get home. But what about Daniel? Give me some *good* news. It was great to hear him and he sounded fairly cheerful but I think he was putting that on a bit."

"He's okay. He looked a bit thinner. I guess he's still pretty worried about everything."

"Of course he would be. What's he going to do? When is he coming home? He wouldn't give me any concrete answers."

"I think he'll be back in a month or two. And he was talking about giving himself up. Perhaps he really did it, Mum."

Mum looked as if I'd hurled the final stone in a barrage that had hit her recently. She was silent for a moment. "How could he?" she asked in a whisper. "Did he actually say he had?"

"Not exactly. I don't understand what's going on with him."

"I can't help feeling I've failed. There must be something I should have done, something I missed."

"It's not your fault, Mum."

"A couple of times I nearly packed up and followed you to Mahaban but I was worried you might be on your way back here and find me gone. Did Casey look after you okay?"

"Perfectly," I said, unable to hide a smile.

"Don't tell me you fell in love with him!"

"What makes you say that?"

"I can see it in your face."

"It's not a disaster, Mum. Don't look at me like that."

"Has he gone back?"

"No. I'm seeing him this evening." I know she was about to tell me I was grounded. "He's leaving tomorrow. Mum, this is our last chance."

"I suppose it's too late to stop you now," she said. Resigned.

If there had been more days, I would have invited Mum to meet Casey, but I couldn't share our last evening.

I showered and put on almost-clean clothes. Even half a day apart had seemed too long. I knew there was going to be a massive gap in me tomorrow, but the warm anticipation of the coming evening was a stronger sensation as the fast twilight fell.

"I missed you," he said in greeting.

Colour clashed with colour. Sound merged with sound. Lights flirted with darkness. People interacted with each other and passed on their way. Through the shifting daily carnival of India, we retraced the steps of our first evening together.

"It's good to finish where we started," Casey said as we dipped into too many dishes.

"You mean this is the end?"

"I can hardly bear to let you go, but do you think we'll both be the same people back in Australia?"

"We could be. But I won't have dust between my toes there." I realised as I said it that the dust in my sandals of yesterday had been replaced by congealed black dirt created by exotic city debris and humidity. It still seemed far preferable to school socks and lace-up shoes.

"Let's not think about that now. I know I won't be able to keep away from you for long. I'll visit you in Australia. That's a promise."

For a few minutes the talk of parting dispersed the glow

of closeness, but slowly it surrounded us again and the reality of the world retreated.

We lingered as long as we could before the inevitable moment outside the hotel gate. Goodbye was tough. "I'll see you soon, sweet Hannah," he said, lips brushing lips one more time. He didn't turn round as he walked into the crowds. The evening air that a minute before had held warmth and a familiar body was suddenly full of empty space.

She throws herself down on the hotel bed. Grey blanket is rough against face wet with tears. Hundreds of traffic horns make monotonous music in the scarcely sleeping city and someone's TV wails songs in Hindi.

TWENTY-SIX

The rest of the time in India was a time of waiting. We found a good swimming pool at one of the big international hotels and went there every day, apart from a couple of days when Delhi Belly hit me again. Both Mum and I were preoccupied with our own wounds but we tried to make the most of the remaining holiday with as much cheerfulness as we could. Actually, despite everything, Mum couldn't help enjoying herself most of the time — I think this was the biggest adventure she'd had in years.

For me, everything was a reminder of Casey.

I nurtured a small hope that he might decide to come back and see me again before we left, but there was no word from him. I took rolls of photos, desperately wanting to capture something of India to take home, trying to put thousands of fleeting impressions into a few representative frames. Packing my bag and getting in the taxi for the airport were the lowest moments. The final goodbye to India. The final goodbye to somewhere that had given life to dusty-footed Hannah. Though its magic wasn't as potent without my fellow traveller, there had been some comfort in the fact that our feet were both touching the earth of the same hot land; that the same breeze might have blown over his body before it reached mine.

In the aeroplane everything melted away behind me — an elaborate ice sculpture left in the sun.

Hours later, Australia was another time, another place, another galaxy. Familiar home was too familiar. For some reason, the half-used toiletries stacked in the shower rack made my heart sink. I was back and nothing had changed in this small world.

And within a day or two it was as if India had been a dream. Occasional physical reminders — dust in the bottom of my bag and the fresh-air and spice smell of the cheesecloth dress — jolted me back, so that, for a moment, I could almost taste an Indian kiss. But, though in many ways my life looked little different from when I had left it, I was no longer the same person living it.

Before I had totally lost the residue of spice in my nostrils, Jody came to breathe India's breath secondhand, to hear tales of Indian nights and Indian days, of Daniel and a distant home in the high hills.

And it was only ten days after we got back that Dad moved out. "A temporary separation," Mum said, "while we reassess our lives." I suppose it wasn't much of a shock. They'd hardly spoken since we got back from India and Dad was finding reasons to stay at work until late in the evening. A year ago it would have stunned me, but now I was beginning to suspect that all solid structures were made of sand and liable to dissolve in the wind.

With both Daniel and Dad gone, life was peaceful but seemed to have lost its purpose. Mostly Mum and I ate in front of the TV instead of at the table. A daily diet of murder and rape with spaghetti, or comedy repeats with microwaved pies. And Marina Trott reporting on the "teenage tenants from hell" or "our children given hard drugs at pocket-money prices". If I did any homework at all, I did it in front of the TV too — something which had never been allowed in our family. Not that I was interested in the programs, but it gave the house a focal point — sort of like tribal people sitting around a camp fire.

A number of times I thought of phoning Melissa and asking her if there was any news from India, but I felt a little wary of her now that she was The Poet's messenger, and I always convinced myself it wasn't the right moment to call.

I wrote pages to Casey over the first couple of weeks but everything I wrote sounded too sentimental. In the end, I pared it down to something simple and chatty.

The highlight of the next few weeks was when my photographs of India were developed. They stirred up mixed feelings for me, but Ms Simone was impressed.

"You've really got something here, Hannah. A fresh eye. I love this series. There's colour, form, movement, space — you've captured it all. Have you considered some sort of artistic career?"

"I haven't thought much further than uni, and since India I don't even feel sure about that."

"I know you have lots of options. If you want some extra encouragement with your photographic skills, I have a friend who runs a TAFE evening course. He's brilliant. You'd love him. They've asked him to run a full-time career course next year."

"I don't think I'd have the time with all the study I need to catch up on."

"It's only one evening a week. Anyway, I'd like to put some of these photos in the 'Youth Perspectives' exhibition in a couple of months. I'm helping organise a showcase of the Gold Coast's best young photographers. I think a series of eighteen would work. Three panels, six on each. I'd say definitely six of these, and some of those abstract fabric stacks. Which others do you think?"

I felt as if I'd resurfaced after a month of swimming through grey soup. Jody phoned that evening.

"We need volunteers at the warehouse. Mark says you're a great worker. He's giving me a lift down from Brisbane on Saturday. We could pick you up on the way if you like."

I needed no further convincing. It would be great to be with friends again.

Friday night, I sorted through all my clothes looking for something that was old enough to work in but good enough that I wouldn't look a total dag. Jeans seemed right, but all my tops seemed to have a flimsy fashion feel about them. They were pre-India Hannah and I hadn't yet developed a look for post-India. Eventually I found an old black T-shirt among the things Daniel had left behind and threw it in the washing machine to remove the slightly stale smell of a year's storage.

Mark and Jody arrived in an old orange VW kombi which threatened to run out of steam on every upward slope. It wasn't the sort of vehicle you could take yourself seriously in and we were more like kids setting off on a picnic than adults about to found a new spiritual centre.

The old warehouse was tucked behind some run-down shops not far from a busy road bridge. At the back of it, the river shone like polished dark wood in the early winter sun.

Inside, it was cavernous and smelt of grain. Shafts of sunlight from high windows illuminated dust particles and never reached the floor. At the far end, half a dozen people were sitting on wooden crates with cups of coffee. Matt, the guard who'd blocked our way on my first visit to the house in India, got up and hugged me. "Hannah! Welcome! Work hasn't been the same without you! Coffee?" Before I could answer, Lena also hugged me like a long-lost relation. "It's great you came, Hannah."

Mark found crates for us then Lena offered to show us round before our coffee arrived.

We went up some open wooden steps to a gallery area

which overlooked the main warehouse floor on three sides. There were three empty rooms which smelt of the ghosts of old files. "These will be offices for Lennox and one for me, and a room where Melissa can relax and receive Guidance. The plan so far is that the main area will be a meditation space, once we've put some softer flooring down. Watch your head on that pulley."

Back downstairs, she showed us the kitchen area and toilets and another office area. "We were so lucky to find this place. We've had a couple of big donations which will easily cover the redecoration and furnishing. We can even pay to have the flooring done professionally, but the rest of the work we'll do ourselves. Its-Supreme-Mysteriousness has really looked after us well."

"Have your coffee, then you can make a start in the offices upstairs. Hayley will be back with some more buckets in a minute."

It didn't have quite the glamour of working on the old house in India, but it was pleasantly familiar to be with these people again and I felt more energetic than I had in weeks. Three of us were working in each room and comments were shouted backwards and forwards between the "teams" who were competing to see who'd be the first finished.

By lunchtime, all the preparation work in the three offices was done. Hayley, who hadn't been in India but was obviously a trusted helper, was sent out to get pizza for all of us.

"Is Troy back from India?" I asked while we extracted slices of pizza with trailing strings of cheese from the open box on a crate table.

Lena immediately donned her role as official public relations spokesperson. "Troy finds it very difficult to be a team player," she said. "He wants to stick with his own interpretation of The Poet's teaching, even though we are fortunate enough to have someone who can constantly give us fresh guidance direct from The Poet. Troy means well but his ego gets in the way."

"How soon before we're open to the public?" another guy asked.

"In about three weeks, I hope. We will have a celebration and blessing as soon as we can. Do all of you know about the gold robes?"

Most of us shook our heads.

"It was Lennox's idea that we should have gold robes for meditation and special occasions — The Poet always said it was a colour of high vibrations. Melissa got the okay from The Poet. They'll be simple to make for anyone with a sewing machine."

"And those of us without?" Jody asked.

"Perhaps someone else would make yours. Do you have a sewing machine Hannah?"

"There's one at home "

"Great. I'll have the bulk fabric here next weekend and give you enough for yourself and Jody. I'll be getting some made up for people, but that'll work out more expensive."

We were about to get back to work when Lena took me aside. "Lennox wants to talk to you later," she said. "He'll be here about four."

"Why me?"

"Nothing to worry about. Probably about Daniel. Hey, we could do your Tribe membership ceremony when we have the opening celebration. That would be an auspicious day for you! You might think it's a bit soon, but you feel like one of us already and you deserve a really good celebration after all your hard work. Don't look so worried; you don't have to do anything difficult. We've got another couple of people joining the Tribe that day so you wouldn't be alone."

In a way it made sense. I'd read and re-read The Poet's book until I thought of him as a wise old friend. And the most important people in my life were Tribe members. But what would my school-friends say? And what about Mum and Dad? Perhaps I didn't even need to tell them. It would be virtually impossible to convince them that this wasn't a "cult" and that I wouldn't be in danger, especially after all that had happened with Daniel.

I was still thinking about it when Lena came to get me for my appointment with Lennox.

He closed the door to his office and pointed to one of the two chairs. He had the "confident and in-control" look of a company director, although his office was almost bare.

"Good to see you again, Hannah. I hear you've been working well, and Lena says you'll be joining the Tribe soon."

"Well, I haven't totally decided yet."

"I'm sure you have the sensitivity to understand The Poet and we'd all love to have you as one of us. But that isn't why I wanted to see you today. It's about Daniel. I'm worried about him. Have you had any news?"

"He's still in India. I'm not sure how he is."

"The Tribe looks after all its members and it's very important we stay united against the rest of the world. Let me show you something." He took out a copy of the previous day's local paper and opened it to the letters page. A letter had been circled in highlighter.

Dear Editor

Why has Council given permission for a cult to use premises in River Street? These people with their brainwashing techniques are a danger to our children and an insult to Christians. Local people should be warned that cults are without morals and that members of this particular cult were recently involved in violence and the serious injury of a young woman. We must fight this threat in whatever way we can. Australia is a Christian country and those who don't like it should go elsewhere.

"And," Lennox continued when I'd finished reading, "this was pushed under the warehouse door last night." He handed me a typewritten sheet of paper.

WE DO'NT WANT YOU HERE. THINGS WILL GET VERY
UGLY. GET OUT NOW. BEFORE ITS TO LATE.

"Probably cranks," I said. "They can't even spell."

"We can't be too careful, Hannah. Any one of us who says
the wrong thing to outsiders or who acts without considering
the Tribe is putting us all at risk. But I'm sure we can rely on
you. And remember to tell me whenever you have news of
Daniel or when he plans to come back."

"*If* he tells us — he might just turn up."

"Remember, we all care about Daniel and about you. Just
let me know whatever you can. Ask Lena for my mobile
number and call me any time. And I hope you'll join us
officially as a Tribe member soon." He touched my arm lightly
and smiled.

Thoughts about becoming a Tribe member resurfaced during quiet moments on Sunday and Monday. I really loved what
I'd read of The Poet. I liked most of the people. But did I want
to be a member of a group the outside world thought of as a
cult? If I put that word to the back of my mind, I had to admit
that I already felt a sense of *belonging* with these people. And
I didn't seem to belong anywhere else these days.

I thought about what Lennox had said too. Before today, I
wouldn't have guessed that he was concerned about Daniel.
It was good to know someone else cared about him.

On Monday an aerogram arrived from Daniel himself.
There was no news of his return. His poem said more than
his short letter:

A hot plains wind
Howls through my hands
Leaving nothing to hold onto
It collects petals from a deity
Dung-dust and discarded days
It dances with palm fronds and plastic
Paper and lightweight dreams
Flinging them at mud walls

Along deserted pathways
Through roadless villages
Whipping grit into eyes and skin
Searching the land
For weak souls to suck dry
Women draw coloured veils across faces
Men squint, squatting close to the ground
Wind with fire in its breath
Hot plains wind
In a strange land
Relentlessly pursues and sears
Extracts tears and devours them
Leaving me
Empty.

TWENTY-SEVEN

"What happens at the Tribe initiation ceremony?" I asked Mark and Jody on the way home from the following Saturday's work marathon.

"It's a symbolic thing," Mark explained, leaning forward to encourage the Kombi up a hill. "You take seven steps towards The Poet ... Well, I don't know what happens now The Poet isn't there. We used to take seven steps towards him and make the seven promises of the Tribe."

"Which are?"

"To give up our attachment to our families, to give up our attachment to material things, to give up our attachment to achievement, to follow the teachings of The Poet, to live our lives with love, to live our lives with awareness, and to put the needs of the Tribe before our personal needs."

"I don't think I want to give up my family." Not that there's much left to give up, I thought.

"You don't have to give up your family, just give up the *attachment* to your family. In other words, be a free individual. You take on the larger family of the Tribe, which is a more natural grouping for humans than the isolated units we've become. It doesn't mean that you can't enjoy your family or

▲ 157

material things or achievement — just that you should put your spiritual integrity before all else."

"And what about all this gold robes stuff ? It sounds a bit strange."

"I suppose we might as well go along with it. I think there'll be some resistance though. Some of us guys aren't so keen to float around like Christmas angels! I wish you could have met The Poet himself. He was what all this is about."

"Somehow I don't think he'd have bothered with the gold robes number," Jody added. "You don't have to sew mine, Hannah. Lena seems to think I'm a charity case."

"I don't think I'll do my own either." The last flare of sun disappeared behind the twilight grey hills ahead. "Apart from anything else, Mum will think I've lost the plot."

Perhaps Mum wouldn't even have noticed, or would have thought I was sewing a graduation gown or a nativity costume out of season. She had been preoccupied with her own thoughts since Dad left.

When I arrived back from the warehouse that day, she'd had her hair cut. Not her usual trim but a new, more geometric look with a streak of chestnut too. She looked bolder, braver, younger.

"Spending the family fortune at the hairdressers now?" I teased. "It looks good."

"Thanks. I went to see your dad this afternoon."

"How's he doing?"

"Pretty miserable, I think. He mainly talked about his new website."

"Is he coming back?"

"Not yet. We can afford two places for a few months while we sort out what's best."

"How will it get sorted out if he won't talk about it?"

"That's what I said to him."

That weekend I was painting at the warehouse on Sunday as well as Saturday. Gradually more and more Tribe members were appearing from somewhere. We got heaps of work done and the place smelt fresher too — I could imagine it being turned into a trendy art gallery. Sometimes I still felt like a newcomer in a strange sect of Poet fanatics, but most of the time I felt at home; that I was part of what we were creating.

By the time the warehouse was nearly ready, I knew I was ready too. My resistance to joining the Tribe had been mostly a superficial one of wondering what outsiders would think of me. And, as the Tribe members had become closer friends than my friends at school, outsiders' opinions became less and less important. I was also longing to see The Poet for myself. There was a picture of him in the book, but everyone said he was even more impressive in real life. I was still a little worried about the "giving up attachment" bit and about "putting the Tribe before my personal needs", but Mark said that simply *trying* to live up to that ideal was enough. No one could be expected to break lifelong habits overnight.

I didn't tell Mum of course. I knew she wouldn't understand and would think she was losing me as well as Daniel and Dad. She had noticed I wasn't around much at weekends and I was always telling half-truths about being out with Jody.

"Are you excited?" Jody asked as we chugged towards the big celebration.

"Terrified!"

"I wish Daniel could be here to see you!"

"Me too. And Casey."

The total metamorphosis of the warehouse took me by surprise even though I'd been involved in its transformation. Since the previous weekend, all the lighting and soft furnishings had arrived, and now it looked like cross between the inside of a church and a Freedom furniture showroom. Two lines of tall uplighter lamps created an aisle down the centre of the main space. At the far end there were was a throne-like chair, and behind that another more elaborate chair on a dais. On a low coffee table beside the throne there were half a dozen folded robes, waiting for those of us who would soon receive them. Around the darker perimeter of the hall, there were rugs and about fifty floor cushions. But the weirdest thing was seeing everyone in gold robes. Those ordinary people I'd come to know and like and laugh with, people who were familiar in jeans and overalls, had changed into awesome figures like elders in a science fiction movie. For a moment I wanted to dash in the opposite direction, but Jody was beside me, encouraging me towards Lena's office.

"So you're ready for your significant moment?" Lena asked.

I nodded.

"Okay. Just fill in this form so we have your details for our records."

I answered all the questions that you'd find on any official form — name, address, telephone number, date of birth and a few others about previous religions and creative/work skills. Then I signed the declaration that said I was taking Tribe membership of my own free will. I handed it back to her and she glanced over it as if it was all routine, but then looked worried.

"You're under eighteen?" she said.

I didn't want it broadcast but I nodded.

"I'm not sure you can legally sign this then. We might need a parent's permission."

"Hey, *we* never had to sign forms," Jody said.

"Lennox very wisely suggested we keep proper records. You never know when we may need to prove things to people who are looking for a reason to destroy us."

"Couldn't I just witness that she is doing this of her own free will?" Jody suggested.

"I think I should refer this to Lennox." At that point two others who were having their initiation ceremony arrived and she relented. "Okay, I suppose so. I don't want to hassle Lennox with details tonight. We may have to make some technical distinction though and call Hannah a probationary member to be verified when she is eighteen."

Jody scrawled a couple of sentences and a signature on a blank bit of paper and Lena stapled it to my form. "Don't worry about it," Jody whispered to me once we were beyond Lena's domain. "Forms are bullshit. This is between you and Its-Supreme-Mysteriousness."

Slowly the cushions filled with people. Jody sat beside me, looking like an Egyptian queen in her gold robe.

When the hall was almost full, Lennox took his seat at the end of the aisle. He was wearing a gold robe and a gold cloak. After a few minutes he stood and raised his hands for silence. A deep quiet instantly swept the last words from people's lips. Then Melissa was there. Melissa like I could hardly have imagined her, regal in a flowing white gown trimmed with gold, her wavy red hair loose like a shawl around her shoulders. She walked with slow, conscious steps to the dais, smiling slightly, seemingly in a world of her own. Adjusting her gown, she sat down slowly and closed her eyes, settling into statue-like stillness.

Lennox spoke. "Welcome to you all, dear brothers and sisters. Through the grace of Its-Supreme-Mysteriousness and the guidance of The Poet, we are all together again in this wonderful new venue. Our time apart was only a time of testing and now we have the means to spread the word to all who want to hear it. Tonight we will have a short meditation, followed by the ceremony to welcome six new Tribe members. Then of course there will be some celebration food, and time to talk to all the people in this special family that you haven't seen for a while. Those of you that were with us at Miralee will realise what an important warning we have received from what happened there. We need no further proof that society and the media will never understand us. They don't *want* to understand us. They would rather stick with their prejudices than find out the truth. But they cannot stop us. Already we have moved from our isolated haven into this new location where we are accessible for many more people. I hope all of you will remember your vow to put the Tribe's needs before your own, and that you will give whatever you can of your time and money to help our work here, so we can take The Poet's words to all those people who are ready to transform their lives."

I had managed to come this far without doing a proper meditation and I wasn't quite sure what to expect. Lennox talked us through relaxing our body and then we were on our own in silence. It didn't do anything special for me but I think I was too nervous about the ceremony.

I was the first to be called and I felt almost naked standing in the glowing aisle without a robe.

Step by step. "I promise to give up attachment to my family." Another step. "I promise to give up attachment to material things." Another step. "I promise ..." Finally, "I promise to put the needs of the Tribe before my own." My steps had been too small and I surreptitiously took an extra one to reach Lennox. He put the gold robe over my head.

"Welcome, Sister. You are now a member of the Tribe. We are your new family and we are here to help you reach your full potential. We expect your loyalty in all things as we will give you ours." He kissed me on both cheeks.

As I moved back to my cushion, the next new initiate was making his way down the aisle. "I promise ..."

The party afterwards was like an enormous shared birthday party. Everyone I even half-knew came up to hug me and say "welcome" after the ceremony. I couldn't remember ever having been the centre of so much attention. My only regrets were that Casey was so far away and that Daniel wasn't there to share the moment and to realise that we were now a part of the same family again. A tribal family.

TWENTY-EIGHT

Its-Supreme-Mysteriousness works in unexpected ways, as we Tribe members are keen on saying.

For a couple of weeks I felt peaceful, pleased to be part of the Tribe — even the longing for Casey had reduced to just a dozen tugging thoughts each day — but perhaps I was just being given time to catch my breath before the next wave of events crashed into me.

It started well, with a phone call.

A woman's voice: "Could I speak to Daniel Jarvis, please."

"I'm sorry, he isn't living here at the moment. This is his sister."

"Can you tell me where I can contact him."

"He isn't really contactable. Who am I speaking to?"

"This is Elaine, Jessica's mother."

"Jessica?"

"Yes, Jessica who was the victim of the shooting. She was a member of the New Tribe."

"Oh, sorry, I didn't think for a minute."

"Jessica is conscious again. It's been so long. The doctors were preparing us for the worst but we've all been praying, refusing to give up hope, and our prayers have finally been answered. She's asking for Daniel. She really wants to see him."

"Daniel is overseas and I can't tell you where he is. I'm so sorry about what happened to Jessica. I mean …"

"Jessie is still a little confused about what happened, but she insists that Daniel didn't hurt her, despite what the police are saying. She wants to thank him for saving her."

"What do you mean?"

"She hasn't said much, but I think she is suggesting that Daniel saved her from being killed. The police are interviewing her this afternoon. I'll phone you again this evening, if you like."

Had I really heard right? Dancing with joy was an option. Or bawling with relief. Despite everything, perhaps the sun was about to shine on us again. I was desperate to tell Mum but she was out doing the supermarket shop. I had to tell someone.

I called a taxi and paced the kitchen until it came. Within twenty minutes I was at the warehouse.

"You're too late to volunteer today," Lena greeted me. "Or are you here for the meditation later?"

"There's something I want to tell Jody. Is she around?"

"I think she already left, but Mark's still here somewhere."

The warehouse was quieter now that all the major renovations were finished, but there were usually a few volunteers cleaning, or keeping an eye on visitors, or doing other odd jobs that Lena always seemed able to find.

Mark was in the kitchen putting up new shelves. "I hear Casey will be back soon," he said, as soon as he saw me.

"Will he? When? I haven't heard anything." Two bits of good news within an hour! I was buzzing with excitement.

"A couple of weeks I think. I got an aerogram on Friday."

"That's amazing. And I just heard that Jessica is conscious again and her mother says it wasn't Daniel."

"Fantastic! Have you told Lennox?"

"No, not yet. I was hoping Jody was here. I wanted to tell her first."

"She's gone house-hunting — you know she wants to move nearer — but she'll be back later. Fantastic news about Daniel! Let's tell Lennox. It's great timing — Melissa's here too. She's been receiving Guidance and they're preparing Lennox's talk for tomorrow."

Did I hesitate for a moment? Did some inner voice say "no" before I let Mark take over. Did I glimpse a shadowy premonition that disappeared as soon as I focused on it?

"Come on," he said, taking my hand and hurrying me back to Lena.

"Lena, Hannah has some great news. Can we see Lennox?"

"What is it?"

"A surprise. Lennox and Melissa should be the first to know."

Lena looked annoyed at being excluded. "Wait a minute. I'll see if he can see you." She phoned up to Lennox. "He'll see you in a few minutes."

"Lennox is looking so radiant recently." Mark whispered as we went up the stairs. "It's since he's been working closely with Melissa and the Guidance. You're lucky to get to talk to him — he's so busy most of us hardly see him. I'll wait with you until he's ready."

Did a small voice try to struggle out of me and speak its unformed doubt while we sat on the sofa beneath the warm spotlight? I do remember thinking, "If it wasn't Daniel, then who was it?"

Lennox opened his door and beckoned me in. Did my feet resist for a split second, trying to tell me something too subtle for my mind? If they did, I urged them on, unheeding.

Lennox *was* looking radiant. The radiance of power. The radiance of being in control. The radiance of being respected as The Poet's right-hand man. But it's easy to say that in retrospect.

"You've got news of Daniel?" he asked.

"Sort of." Did my tongue hover, unwilling, before the words burst through? No, they tumbled out eagerly. "I had a phone call from Jessica's mother. Jessica is conscious again and she says Daniel didn't do it. He'll be able to come back."

Did I know then that I'd let loose the words that would give him the vital warning? That I was a careless Pandora who opened the box and released invisible things? That within a very short time I would want to recapture them and lock them up where Lennox would never hear them? If I knew, it was an unfamiliar knowing; a primitive voice that spoke without words, as a rabbit's instinct might speak when a concealed predator has it within its sight.

Lennox didn't look happy. "I see." He stood up and went to the window, his eyes searching the street below. "When did you hear this?"

Could I have saved the situation at that point? Should I have read a change of tone or the flicker of his eye? Could I still have protected us by spinning some speedy lies? "Only about half an hour ago. It will take ages to get a letter to Daniel, but at least the police will know the true story."

"What else did Jessica say?"

"I don't know. Her mother won't tell me much until Jessica has talked to the police. They're probably with her now."

Would I have told him more if I'd known more? Probably. He cared about Daniel, didn't he?

"You've done well to get here so quickly to tell me. Your loyalty to the Tribe is impressive. This is important news. But things are not as straightforward as you think. We have many enemies out there and the police aren't going to give up a chance to destroy us."

"What do you mean?" The tone of his voice told me more than the words. And that was the first moment I was really conscious of having trodden where no angel would have been dim-witted enough to tread.

"There was a good reason why the shooting happened, but outsiders won't understand that. And if Daniel is cleared, we are all in danger. Everything we have worked for here will fall apart."

"I don't understand."

"I must consult with Melissa and get Guidance. Please stay in the warehouse and don't say anything about this to anyone. I will make an announcement in a minute. Tell Lena to come here immediately."

I walked back down the wooden stairs, replaying the scene in my head, searching for clues that would make sense of Lennox's response. Lena was still in the reception area.

"Lennox wants to see you, immediately," I told her, hoping she might be able to contain whatever danger Lennox had foreseen.

"Just watch the desk for a minute then," she said. "And answer the phone if it rings."

I sat at the desk and fiddled with pens, fingertips getting sweaty. The phone didn't ring.

Within minutes Lena was back. She rushed past me and bolted the front door.

Then she clapped her hands like a kindergarten teacher calling for quiet. "Everyone sit down," she shouted. "Lennox has an important announcement to make."

TWENTY-NINE

As we all settled on cushions, exchanging questioning glances, Lennox and Melissa appeared at the top of the stairs.

"This is very important," Lennox announced from his platform above us. "The Tribe is under threat. Some members of the Tribe have been working against us. There is a good chance the police will arrive here soon to question us again. As your leader, it is likely they will target me particularly. Make no mistake: they want to destroy us and they will do that by destroying me first. In a minute we will leave. I may have to go into hiding for a while for the good of all of us. As you know, Daniel's fingerprints were on the gun that wounded Jessica, but it seems, because they were lovers, she has concocted a story to try to clear him. If the police question you, remember your loyalty to the Tribe. You don't have to tell them anything. Once Melissa and I have left, Lena will unlock the front door and you can all go home. In the meantime ..."

Before he could finish, someone rattled the front door handle and then knocked loudly.

No one spoke. Lennox nodded urgently towards Lena. "Who is it?" she called out.

"The police. We want to see Lennox Escott and ask him a few questions."

Lena looks at Lennox. Lennox looks frantically in every direction like a cornered animal.

"He's not here," Lena shouts.

"Can we come in and talk to you?" the male voice asks, more of a command than a question.

Lennox grabs Melissa's hand and hurries her down the stairs towards the fire exit at the far end of the hall. As he opens it, I see a police car and a couple of police in the car park. Quickly he slams it shut again and rams the security bolts in place.

He flees back up the stairs.

He lets go of Melissa and pulls a gun from his briefcase. "You can't come in. I have hostages!" he yells.

The rest of us freeze, uncomprehending.

Next, Lennox aims at one of the high windows and the glass shatters as the shot sounds. A few shards fall to the floor behind us.

"Take it easy!" the policeman yells. "We just want to talk to you. We're not coming in. Is anyone hurt?"

"I'm not talking. BACK OFF!"

"Don't do anything silly, mate. We're not forcing anything, okay?" There is concern and urgency in the shouted command now.

Lennox doesn't answer. The rest of us sit like wax dummies. He waves the gun backwards and forwards in an arc across the group, as if waiting for someone to break ranks.

Outside, the muffled sounds of police radios. Traffic passing.

A minute passes. Two. Maybe five. Seems like a month. Then the sound of more cars arriving at the front and rear of the building.

The phone rings and we all levitate in unison. We'd

thought we were tensed to breaking but the sound tightens us another notch.

Lennox motions Lena towards the phone with a wave of his gun.

"Warehouse Meditation Centre," Lena says, only a slight tremor indicating this is not a normal afternoon at the office. "It's the police for you, Lennox."

"Tell them they've got until midnight to leave our premises. Tell them this is religious persecution."

She repeats his words and pauses. Listens. Says a "yes", then a "no", then, "They want to talk to you, Lennox."

"I'm not talking. Now get the hell off that phone."

Lena replaces the phone.

It rings again. She waits, looking to Lennox for further instructions.

"Unplug it."

The piercing sound is cut off mid-tone, and with it our link to the outside world.

My legs have seized up from sitting awkwardly. My neck feels like steel cable. But I daren't move.

Still we sit in silence. I don't turn to look at faces, but I can see Melissa's, etched with uncertainty, and Lena's, watchful, lion-like.

Minutes stretch to years again. Silence is as solid as iron. Then someone sobs behind me.

Melissa moves forward and whispers to Lennox who never takes his eyes and gun off us.

"It may be a long wait." His voice still holds the command of absolute determination. "You can stretch out. But no one is to move from the cushions without permission."

A communal sigh, slight but audible, escapes as we shift our stiff limbs to new positions.

More minutes pass. Maybe twenty. Maybe thirty. After-noon light fades early to winter darkness.

Melissa whispers to Lennox again and goes into the office.

She returns with a chair. He sits. She gets another one for herself.

Slowly, slowly, notch by notch, the tension is released to about three-quarter stretch.

Beside me a hand raises tentatively. A reluctant student unsure if he's out of line with a question. "May I use the toilet?" he asks.

The toilets are out of sight towards the back of the building. But they have no windows.

Lennox considers for a moment. "Anyone who wants to use the toilets, line up. If anyone tries anything silly, they'll wish they hadn't. I have to protect you all from traitors who might endanger us."

We all move towards the toilets — safety in numbers or all suddenly realising our bladders are feeling the strain — and Lennox follows us at a distance. We stand like pre-school kids waiting out turn with Lennox now watching us from the hall doorway.

Those who have finished stand in a group, waiting for permission to move back to the hall.

When we've all finished, Lennox walks backwards leaving the doorway clear for our return to the cushioned hall.

We settle into more comfortable positions, stretching out for the wait.

Lennox is less strained but still alert. "Mark and Hannah, go to the kitchen and fill all the containers you can find with water. If we have to wait this out, we'll need fresh water and the bastards are likely to cut our supply — or poison it. Remember what happened to innocent people like us in Waco, Texas. We can't be too careful."

Without talking, Mark and I move to the kitchen and do as we are told. I know Lennox can see the kitchen doorway from his perch, but I glance at Mark wondering if his face has anything to say. He looks grim, eyes saying everything and nothing.

"Get back in here as soon as you've done it," Lennox shouts.

We hurry back. Any opportunity is gone before we have the chance to use it.

Another two "volunteers" are sent to make sandwiches for everyone.

When the plates arrive, we pull our cushions into a circle and eat slowly. The bread feels rough against my dry throat and no amount of chewing creates appetite or saliva. Lennox is eating his left-handed, the gun still in his right hand. Lena has switched on the warehouse lights, creating a church-like atmosphere, and beyond the high windows the black of the urban night is infused with amber.

"It's a bit like the Last Supper," Lennox says all of a sudden.

Someone giggles nervously.

Faces are white. Fear and uncertainty gather like the electrical charge before lightning. Sandwiches are left half-eaten.

Then one of the guys gets up and runs toward the back door. "Stop!" shrieks Lennox. His gun swings round to track the fleeing figure.

The guy sinks to his knees with no need for a shot to bring him down. He is shaking.

"No one leaves. We are ALL in this together," Lennox commands.

One again we are all jolted into alertness like puppets jerked by an erratic puppeteer.

"Brothers, sisters, I am not against you," Lennox then says soothingly. "But we have to act as one against the outside world. You know they don't understand us. You know they want to destroy anything that's truly fresh, anything that might make the public wake up from its convenient slumber. We'll let the police sweat it out a bit longer, then I'll reconnect the phone and tell them our demands." He smiles. "Well, make yourselves comfortable but don't move from the cushions, okay?"

Slowly everyone unclenches just enough to take up a long-wait posture.

"Kerri, take the plates back to the kitchen." Lennox instructs one of the girls who made sandwiches. "Then come up here and keep watch out of the window behind me. I will talk to you all about our Master. Then you can spread out and sleep. Lena, bring me Book Two."

Lena takes one of The Poet's books to him and he searches through it for a couple of minutes before speaking again. " 'Love is the ground of our being; love is not merely for our own pleasure'. How many of you remember this quote from The Poet? How many of you seek only the pleasure and would take a new lover if you had an opportunity? How many of you would ignore these words if it suited you? It is obvious that most people are still too weak to uphold this important teaching. Daniel and Jessica went against this divine guidance from The Poet. In fact, Jessica was little more than a whore who has almost destroyed our Tribe. And Daniel was so full of his own ego he put his lust before everything. When we get out of here, there will be new rules. No members of the Tribe will pair up without permission. Those women who fear they may be tempting men will come to me and I will counsel them on how best to deal with their confusion."

Does he really think we will get out of here?

"Lena, I think everyone should put on their robes, just in case anything happens. If we must die for our belief in The Poet, we should die in glory for him."

Lena hands out robes. We put them on. We have no choice.

"Dim the lights, Lena. Try to rest, everyone. Kerri, tell me if you see anything suspicious."

A couple of people reach for extra cushions and lie down. I copy their example. I close my eyes but there are too many thoughts for sleep. The one that comes round most often is wishing I hadn't said anything to Lennox. If he hadn't been warned, the door would have been open and the police would have come in before all this could happen. I think about dying and wonder if Lennox is capable of something really crazy. I think about Casey and wish that he was here too. Somehow I would feel safer if he was here. What is the truth of all this? Could The Poet have shot Jessica? Could Daniel and Lennox both be protecting him? Could Lennox's version be true? Or is the person who shot Jessica the one pointing his gun at us? I could almost believe that Daniel would sacrifice himself for The Poet, but I just can't believe that The Poet would be violent. It seems as unlikely as Jesus or Buddha driving a tank. I think about Mum and know she'll be worried about me by now. I shift position and think the same things again with very little variation. Then I go right back to square one and wish Daniel hadn't got us into this mess to start with.

After a while I start thinking about escape strategies, which is pointless as I'd never be brave enough to risk it. So instead I work out the best things to do if there is a shoot-out. Run for the toilet and lock the door? I might be shot as I ran. Hide behind one of the pillars? Not much protection really. Plead? I wouldn't like to gamble that Lennox would listen. Play dead? I'd be an easy target but I might get overlooked if the focus is on the activity. I wonder what everyone will say if I die in a siege. I wonder about the life I would have had. I try to remember what The Poet has said about death. When you don't expect to die for another sixty years, you don't take much notice; but when you realise it could happen in sixty seconds, your perspective changes. I don't sleep but drift deeper into swirling thoughts, further from alertness.

Then suddenly there's a shout from Kerri. "Man on the roof." People leap up, startled. Lennox rises and turns in one movement. Someone screams. Another window explodes in mind-splitting noise.

"If we die, we die for The Poet." Lennox shouts. "People will remember us. People will remember The Poet through our sacrifice."

A ghostlike figure appears behind him. Melissa.

"Lennox, I don't think The Poet would want us to die," she says. Her voice is quiet but our senses are strained, hyper-alert. We hear.

He turns to her with disgust and grabs her arm, holding the gun to her head. "You. How could you of all people betray us?"

A horrified hush falls. No, it is deadly quiet already. But I sense the intake of breath. Someone starts sobbing again. My teeth are sinking into my knuckles but I don't feel the pain.

"STAY AWAY," Lennox hollers into the night.

Melissa, softer and whiter than ever, says, "Lennox, let me get Guidance on this. Remember, The Poet respected life in all its forms. Please let me get Guidance."

"You know you can't always tune in. There's no time now."

"Give me a few minutes. I'm sure it will come through when we really need help."

He lets her go and shoves her towards her room. "Hurry!" He grabs Kerri to replace Melissa. Kerri screams.

Oh, frail, brave Melissa, will you be wise enough to manage this? Will you create some convincing Guidance if none comes through?

The minutes tick by, Lennox as jumpy as a startled race-horse. I cling precariously to self-control. Nails penetrating palms. Scream clamped in throat. Nerves seared.

Melissa appears again.

"The Poet says —" At first her voice is faint. She clears her throat and pushes the words harder. "He needs us to be his spokespeople. He says we cannot fight with force but with wisdom."

"Is that all?" Lennox sounds dismissive, looks deranged.

The flicker of Melissa's eyes tells me she is searching for more, that she's on her own now. "He says his trusted son Lennox should lead us out of hiding into the hearts of many people. That only through surrender will victory be ours."

"Surrender? The ultimate surrender?" Lennox gleams, radiance rising.

"He says throw down your gun and go open-handed into the night."

"You're lying!" Fury.

For a second Melissa looks panic-stricken. Everything hangs in the balance.

Then from her depths a massive voice bypasses her fear: "He says THROW DOWN YOUR WEAPON!"

Lennox is faltering now but still holding onto the gun. His grip on Kerri loosens and she crumples in a heap at his feet.

"THROW DOWN YOUR GUN!" Melissa is expanding, sucking the radiance from Lennox.

His posture is softer but he still holds the gun. Melissa puts her arm through his. "Come," she commands. "We must lead these people to safety. It's what The Poet wants." Indecision struggles on in him but Melissa is committed now, watching like a warrior for an opponent's faltering moment. Within seconds she has seized it. "Lead us, Lennox," she says, leading *him* down the stairs. We all shuffle back a few centimetres. When they are near the door, he holds back. They are right beside me. Lennox is close enough to touch me. Melissa is on his left. I feel my body cold, clammy; dryness burns my throat.

"Put the gun down, Lennox. We need to go out with our hands up," Melissa says. He still hesitates. His right hand is holding the gun more loosely now. Just for a second his arm drops a little.

Melissa's eyes momentarily fix on mine.

I thrust my body upwards clumsily. I grab the gun. I don't even think. I just know this is the only moment. Although I move fast, everything happens in slow motion. I'm sure he will see what is happening long before I reach him, but he turns in slow motion too. I don't want the heavy thing, still warm from his hands. But I cling onto it and step backwards, crushing my cushion and almost stumbling. My arms are trembling, my legs are quaking but my feet still find the floor.

As shock hits his face, Melissa is already moving between us. "You don't need it," she says. "Come, Lennox, this is best for The Poet."

He's still unsure but his power is slipping away.

"Your bastard brother and now you!" he half shouts, half cries at me, "You've ruined everything we've all worked for."

Lena dashes to unlock the front doors. "He's coming out. He's not armed," she yells, holding the door open just a little.

"This is our Victory," Melissa says, urging Lennox forward. "We'll be on every TV screen tomorrow. The world will know about The Poet!"

With the doors open, I see the police all around, guns pointing at Lennox.

Mark catches me as my legs melt.

THIRTY

It's not often that two members of the one family have to explain why their fingerprints are on guns they didn't use. A private joke now revolves around "Don't touch it, you'll get fingerprints on it!" Not that it was a joking matter at the time.

We got more attention than the Australian Olympic Team when we emerged from the warehouse, dazed and dazzling in gold robes. TV cameras were running, lights flashed, police were everywhere, and both Mum and Dad were among the crowd that had gathered after the siege had been on the evening news. The familiar figure of Marina Trott was hovering, thrusting her microphone and predictable questions in the faces of dazed victims. *"Were you scared?"*, *"Was there a moment when you thought you might not get out alive?"*, *"It must have been a terrifying experience for you."*

In the first days afterwards, the sheer relief at being alive and the long round of police questioning made everything seem unreal. Only later was there time for the horror to sink in. And it sunk into every cell of my body. It still seeps out sometimes, especially at night when I toss and turn, tangling myself in sheets, or when someone makes a sudden move in a crowded place and every muscle in my body freezes. I don't know if it will ever entirely leave me. A few hours like that can change you forever.

Dad came back home that night. He did his best to reassure me. I was still too shell-shocked for all the words we said to lodge in my memory, but I know he told me things would be okay; that even if he and Mum didn't stay together, he'd still love me and he'd still look out for me.

Within days, the police had charged Lennox with the attempted murder of Jessica. Then Melissa came round to visit. We were both still trying to put together the missing pieces of the story.

"I don't understand Lennox," I said, as we ate chocolate-cherry muffins Mum had baked. "What exactly happened on the night of the shooting?"

"I think only Lennox, Jessica and Daniel know the whole story. Lennox says he didn't mean to hurt her, only to frighten her, but when Daniel grabbed the gun it went off. He'd followed Daniel into Jessica's room, disgusted that she had been flirting with Daniel."

"Why is he *still* trying to put the blame on Daniel? Do you believe him?"

"I don't know what to believe. I want to believe that it was an accident. It freaks me out to think of him as a potential murderer." She paused, wiping a crumb from the corner of her mouth. "Jessica told the police that Lennox was jealous; that he wouldn't let her go. *He* says it wasn't that. He says he was furious with her for not living up to The Poet's teaching and for coming on to every guy in sight." She squashed a stray brown crumb against the white plate. "I could believe either of them. Or both." She pushed back the too-long sleeves of her too-baggy jumper. "Lennox worshipped The Poet like a father. His real Dad left when he was two and never kept in touch. I think he was capable of doing anything to defend The Poet's teaching."

"The end justifies the means ..." I said, remembering

something Casey had said in India. "I can't help thinking what might have happened."

"You were really brave, Hannah. You did the right thing."

"And you. You broke the deadlock."

"I was terrified." She went to take another bite of muffin and stopped. "I just had to do what had to be done. To start with I was begging The Poet, begging Its-Supreme-Mysteriousness, begging for help. Then my body just took over."

"So you invented that Guidance about surrendering."

"Yes. But I knew what The Poet would have said. I knew he wouldn't want us to die in some crazy stand-off."

"And all the other messages before?" I asked, very tentatively.

"I was sure at the time. It was coming through so clearly. Now I wonder if I imagined it. It's very hard being psychic. You have to trust your own experience but in a world where nothing is entirely solid. Remember Joan of Arc?" She was close to tears. "I'm going to stick by him, Hannah. I think his idealism just got a bit out of control."

"A *bit*!"

"He's trying to push me away at the moment. But he needs me. No one else will visit him while he's locked up waiting for trial. It may take ages before the case is even heard. And I don't think his version of the story will carry much weight in court against Jessica's version, but even she admits that she and Daniel were making out."

Outrage tore through me like a dark tornado. "Does that give Lennox the right to shoot her? To let the police blame Daniel? Have you any idea what we've all been through? The siege was nothing compared with what he's done to Daniel and our family. How can you even think of standing by him? He's a maniac!"

"I know he was doing it for The Poet. Sometimes the right ideas have the wrong results."

"You can't just dismiss it like that. By that argument, you can destroy anyone who gets in your way!"

"Hannah, I know it's been hard on you, but would you really want to wipe out the last year? You would never have gone to India, never have met Casey?"

I wanted to continue hurling blame at Lennox but my mind wouldn't sort out a logical argument. Thoughts were easily demolished by emotional reaction in the aftermath of everything. "Did Jody know about Daniel and Jessica?"

"No. Jody wouldn't have stood for that. Do you think she and Daniel are still an item?"

"It's hard to say when he's been away so long."

It wasn't easy to get news to Daniel. Mum and I both sent a separate letter to his next Poste Restante address in India. Mine said simply: "Jessica is conscious and recovering. She has told the police everything and you're in the clear! Phone to find out more. And PLEASE come home soon!" As soon as he received the letters he called us. Even across the echoing phone line, I could tell he was happier than he'd been for a long time. "But why didn't you just tell the police at the beginning that Lennox shot her and that you took the gun from him?" I asked.

"It was his word against mine unless Jessica recovered. He was wearing the disposable gloves we used for cleaning and food preparation. I wasn't, so my prints were the only ones on the gun. It didn't look good. And I didn't want Jody to know I was in Jessica's room that night. I don't think she'll ever forgive me. It wasn't a good move."

"I can't believe you were actually going to take the blame for something you didn't do."

"I was totally confused. I thought it was the best thing for The Poet's work. You know the bit in the vows about putting the Tribe's needs before our own? The Tribe needed Lennox's leadership while The Poet was away. And on another level I was shit-scared of him. He's the main reason I left Mahaban so soon after you arrived. Plus of course I already had a police record …"

"People are saying you're a hero for taking the gun from Lennox."

"I don't feel like one. And Jody won't think so when she hears the full story. There was a good chance I would have cheated on her that night if we hadn't been interrupted. I don't want to make excuses but I can't help wishing I could turn back the clock."

"You and me both. There was a big drama here and it was all my fault. But at least it showed how ruthless Lennox can be, which will be extra evidence when he comes to court." I gave him a brief version of the siege. "I'll tell you all the details when you get back. You will come back soon?"

"As soon as I can get on a flight."

I think we were all waiting for Daniel's return before we could even begin to get back to normal. Not that "normal" would ever be the same as it had been. Dad stayed out of the way a lot, but when he was around he was doing his best to keep the peace.

I don't know how the TV station knew which flight Daniel was on, but Marina Trott was there, a pristine vulture in icy blue.

Every minute waiting in the Arrivals area seemed like a massive chunk of lifetime. Each time the automatic doors slid open it could have been him, but someone else's brother or sister would stride out searching for familiar faces among the waiting crowd.

Then he was there. For a moment he stood still, only half-smiling, then we all moved at once. "Hi guys," he said, his voice muffled by hugs. "Sorry it took so long. The police intercepted me at immigration. Just a few questions for now, but they needed to know where they could find me later for a full statement. It's great to see you all!"

The TV cameras got their moment of emotion. We couldn't have hidden it if we'd tried.

We watched their story later that evening.

"Nineteen-year-old Daniel Jarvis arrived back in Brisbane today from India following revelations that he has been cleared of suspicion in the shooting incident at the hinterland premises of the cult The New Tribe. Lennox Escott, who was working closely with the charismatic cult leader known as "The Poet" has now been charged with the attempted murder of Jessica Vellucci and is facing a number of charges relating to the recent siege at the cult's Gold Coast centre. Jessica's mother was full of praise for Daniel's action which may have saved Jessica from a more serious fate. Daniel himself declined to comment, but a former girlfriend and cult member said the heroic action was what she would have expected from Daniel. The camera cuts to Jody: 'Daniel is the sort of guy who would just act without thinking about his own danger. I wasn't surprised to hear he was a hero.'

Daniel's sister Hannah was also in the news recently when she disarmed Escott during the siege at the New Tribe's Gold Coast headquarters. The brother and sister are being dubbed "the Cultbuster Twins" (old footage of me in my robe emerging from the warehouse looking like a bewildered angel expelled from heaven). *Meanwhile investigations continue into the cult and its leader who is believed to be in hiding overseas. In other news today, employment figures are up again, work begins on the new Megaplex shopping centre, another top model admits she has anorexia, and how a new drug designed for low blood pressure brings unexpected benefits for your sex life."*

"Cultbuster Twins!" Daniel laughed scornfully.

"First I'd heard of it," I said.

"Seriously, thanks all of you," Daniel said. "It's great to be back."

Dad stood up and turned the TV off. "It's good to have you home, Dan," he said. "You're a hero, mate. I know we haven't always seen eye to eye —" He was struggling for a foothold, an explorer in new territory. "I guess things have been pretty tough for you." Dad was shifting uneasily from leg to leg and, for the second time in the day, Daniel wiped the heel of his hand across his eyes. "But we're proud of you. How about a beer to celebrate?"

Mum dashed for the fridge with the sort of smile I thought her face muscles had forgotten. "Both you kids are going to need plenty of rest and some peace and quiet to recover from all this," she said. "Your Dad and I still have things to sort out together but we've agreed not to let them get in your way over the coming weeks. When Ross arrives for his visit next week, we'll have another celebration — the first time we've all been together for two years!"

"The offer of a computer job is still open," Dad said to Daniel. "Only if you're interested, of course."

"I've been thinking I might go back and do Year 12, so I can go to uni — that's if I can still live here."

"Of course," Mum said. "I'm going to do a nursing degree part time and I think Hannah will have to repeat, so we'll all be studying together."

It didn't seem the moment to tell them that school seemed as appealing as a wet weekend in the Christmas holidays. I couldn't imagine how I'd ever study again. I was planning to find out about the full-time TAFE photography course that Ms Simone's friend was starting.

"Thanks for everything, Hannah," Daniel said to me later. "It's good to know someone believed in me."

"Well, there were times I wasn't sure."

"But Casey told me you never gave up."

"I couldn't help that! You're my brother! Have you called Jody yet? She was your chief defender."

"She called herself *former* girlfriend on the TV."

"But you should phone her anyway."

"Do you think she'll forgive me? All the sordid details will come out at the trial, even if the press don't get there first."

"Fifty-fifty, I'd say. She won't be a pushover, that's for sure."
I hesitated a minute. "What was — is — Jessica like?"

"I don't know. She's one of those people who's always smiling and doesn't seem to get bogged down in problems. I think that was what attracted me. That, and her body, I have to admit. There's heaps I didn't know about her, but she seemed to glide easily through life, you know? I thought about it endlessly while I was away. I was getting scared of the relationship with Jody. I longed for her but didn't know how to keep hold of her. One moment she was in the palm of my hand and life was amazing, the next she'd get all elusive on me. She's so fiercely independent it's scary sometimes. No one teaches you how to handle difficult women! Jessica suddenly looked enticingly uncomplicated. But it was Jody I wanted to be with all those months in India, though I worried heaps about Jessica and what had happened."

"So will you call Jody?"

"When I'm feeling brave enough."

"You're the brave hero, remember?"

"There's bravery and bravery!"

Two days later Casey came back. First there was his phone call. We'd been leaving the phone off the hook quite a bit and I was preparing our standard rejection for the journalists trying to get an interview with the "Cultbuster Twins".

She answers the phone with sandwich in hand. Tries to sound cool, swallowing a mouthful unchewed. Yes, it would be wonderful if you could come. Yes, Daniel's here too. Yes, two o'clock would be fine.

She changes into clean jeans and fitted shirt. Brushes hair, beautifies face. Hurries too much. Hopes too much.

She counts to ten before opening the door. He sees her. She knows he really sees her, as he saw her in India. But then he puts away those eyes. Substitutes the eyes clouded by the multitude of things that have to be considered.

There's a hug for Daniel and a hug for her. The arms, the touch, the familiar scent. Bodies remember with an intensity minds forget. But he's shielding his senses from the wave of body-memory.

Disappointment, not entirely unexpected, hauls her dreams back to earth. She watches him talking to Daniel, both of them settling among sofa cushions and scattered CDs. Hard to believe he's here, his vibrant form imposed on the familiar domesticity. He stirs the air with every movement. Molecules of India still shimmer on his skin. He sheds them in his wake, not knowing the shock waves they create in the Queensland calm.

I went through the whole story of the siege again for Casey, finding the memories of it less spiky and disturbing the tenth time round. He listened intently, asking a few questions, reassuring me that I wasn't to blame. "I always knew you were one strong woman," he said, after I'd explained the bit about taking the gun from Lennox.

"Maybe," I said, pleased he thought so, even if it had felt more like desperation than strength at the time.

"And have either of you seen Jessica yet?" he asked.

"I spoke to her mother again. Jessica wants Daniel to visit as soon as he's settled enough to know what day it is. She's making excellent progress now she's conscious again."

"I'll go tomorrow. I really worried about her. A mega-weight lifted off me when I got Hannah's letter that she was okay. And not just because it cleared me of the shooting."

"I have some other amazing news for you guys," said Casey, "The Poet is back from his pilgrimage."

"Where is he?" Daniel asked.

"Melbourne at the moment. Troy has spoken to him on the phone."

"Are you sure?" Though phones are more reliable than telepathic messages, I was still dubious.

"Certain. You can trust Troy on that sort of thing. He says The Poet has asked us to give him privacy while he's in

Melbourne but he plans to find a property way out west to continue his work."

"What did he say about all the mess that happened while he was away?" I asked. Since the siege, I hadn't been quite so sure about The Poet, even though it wasn't his fault Lennox had gone over the top, and I was a little surprised to hear Casey still sounding so enthusiastic.

"I don't know. Troy's phonecard ran out while he was talking to me. I only heard this morning. I guess we'll get the full story soon enough."

"So, what are your plans now?" Daniel asked.

"Spend a few days with Mum then I think I'll head down to Sydney to get some work until we get the okay to join The Poet. How about you, Dan? You've had one hell of an experience."

"I still can't believe I'm here and free, but I want to get to uni. I reckon by the beginning of the new year I'll have returned to what passes for sanity. I'm not sure whether I'll have to go back to school or whether I can get in as a mature-age student, but I'll do it somehow."

"You won't join us out west? Troy said Mark is going to drive the kombi out and Jody was excited at the idea of getting back to the spirit of the land."

"I'll come in the vacations if I'm not flat broke. Being in exile gave me time to think about the things that I'd really like to do. Only ordinary things, but I'll appreciate them heaps more because of all the time I thought I'd never get a chance to do them."

Casey looked at me but didn't find a question. I looked at him and didn't find an answer. Daniel understood. "Should I give you two a bit of time alone together?" he asked.

"Well —" Casey's usual, confident control of the situation momentarily slipped through his fingers. "How about I take Hannah out for a coffee?"

"Okay by me," Daniel replied.

"Hannah would need to be consulted," I said.

"Would you like to, Hannah? Just for an hour or so? I'll give you a lift back."

"Sure," I said, sorry that I couldn't think of a more elusive way to say "yes".

He takes her to a café where the first floor is open to an ocean view. She sits beside him so they can both see the ocean. So they can focus on the distance.

"You must come and stay at The Poet's new place sometime," he says. "I know you've had a frightening experience with the Tribe but The Poet is something else."

"I might do that. It's hard to make sense of everything at the moment and I really don't want to study any more. I need something to look forward to."

He puts his hand on hers. "Remember, The Poet says to live each moment as it comes. Make each moment significant."

"I can see the wisdom of that, but don't you think people who have all the answers are a major pain in the backside?"

He smiles and considers. "Yes. Better to hold to the question than accept a regurgitated answer."

Then, with cappuccino lips, he turns to her and says, "I wanted to say thank you."

"For what?"

"Thank you for the beautiful days and nights in India. Being with you took me by surprise. I wanted you to know that it was a very special time for me."

"For me too," she says. "For me too."

Cappuccino lips taste warm and sweet.

Another warehouse, another evening. Yellow lights spills over the pavement, and a turquoise and orange banner says "Youth Perspectives. Photographic Exhibition from Tomorrow's Photographers".

Ms Simone is wearing a short black dress, and is gliding around directing press, proud parents and guests from Gold

Coast galleries. "Go and see your panels, Hannah," she says. "They look even better now they're mounted. They're along that wall at the far end."

Passing the other photographers' work I wonder if mine will measure up. Stark black and white faces ask unanswerable questions, outback townships tell tales of desertion, fashion models sit at plates filled with jewellery and dollar notes, a street-person huddles in the doorway of stylish insurance company offices, a dozen dazed people fill gaping mouths with fast food.

The vibrant images of India take me by surprise.

She stands and stares at the enlarged photos, big enough to step into. The swirling, chattering gallery crowd recedes into a blur behind her.

The taste of India is on her tongue again and she settles into the still eye of the hurricane. She smells the spices, sees the gas lights and saturated colours, hears the cacophony of Bombay streets — the juice wallahs, the marching band, the Asian pop from radios, the constant dull bleats of traffic horns. She breaths in the jasmine and dust on the warm night air and feels his hand on her shoulder.

"I see you brought India home with you," he says. "I had to come along to the Opening Night. Why didn't you tell me about this the other day?"

She turns and smiles. "Yes, I think I did bring India back. And not just in the photos."

THIRTY-ONE

Daniel's Notebook
11 November
I was wounded and wailing;
Bound and blind;
Lost and confused.
I crawled out of my cell
And searched.
Life was more cruel and more gentle than I knew;
Harsher and sweeter than I imagined;
Tougher and more tender than my dreams.
I didn't find heaven
But I found a place to call home;
I didn't find God
But I saw him in the eyes of a man
And felt him in the touch of a woman.
And that,
For now,
Is sufficient.

touch me

James Moloney

"When can I hold you, then?" He whispered. "I want to. I
…" He was going to say *I love you* but what did that mean?

For Xavier McLachlan, Rugby is life. Winning a 1st XV jersey
means everything … Until he meets Nuala Magee. Has there
ever been a girl like her? She's feisty, she's troubled, she's
dangerous. What will his mates think? Does he even care?
Everything looks different now. Xavier McLachlan is in love.

ISBN 0 7022 3151 7

Angela

James Moloney

Angela and Gracey were going to be "best friends forever" and make it into the same university as carefree first year students. But for Gracey, her Aboriginal heritage takes on a new significance.

While Angela falls in love for the first time, Gracey is drawn into black politics and their friendship drifts apart. Then Angela discovers that she too has a heritage — one her family would sooner deny. The conflict of the past possesses the power to draw the friends together but it could as easily blow them apart forever.

This novel concludes the trilogy, which began with award-winning *Dougy* and *Gracey*. James Moloney yet again shows why his novels are so much in demand as powerful narratives of contemporary Australian society.

ISBN 0 7022 3084 7

Wish You Weren't Here

Daryl McCann and Debbie Forbes

"We can't be kids forever," Cam informed her.

"That's right, we can't so why don't you bloody well grow up!"

… People all over the world would soon be slipping effortlessly from one year into another … Becky leaned back in her chair and wished she was one of them.

Becky just wishes some things would stay the way they were. She wants the old friendship she used to have with her best friend Cam. And she wants the lead role in the school play that's always been hers. And most of all she wants her Mum's boyfriend Alwyn, "The Ferret", to get out of their lives.

Wish You Weren't Here is a sharp and darkly humorous story of a fifteen-year-old girl's entry into the grown-up world of expectation, lust and not always getting what you want.

ISBN 0 7022 3103 7

The Heroic Lives of Al Capsella

Judith Clarke

The popular series that elevates ordinariness to cult status is available for the first time in this one hilarious edition.

Follow the heroic exploits of mild-mannered suburban hero Al Capsella and his mate. Draws on the classic Al Capsella trilogy: *The Heroic Life of Al Capsella*, *Al Capsella and the Watchdogs* and *Al Capsella on Holidays*.

ISBN 0 7022 3061 8

Water Bombs

Steven Herrick

Steven Herrick's free verse is challenging, life-affirming and a delight to savour. In this new edition of his first book of poetry for young people are previously unpublished poems that extend and celebrate the poet's perceptions of everyday life.

ISBN 0 7022 3162 2

The Simple Gift

Steven Herrick

"What can I say. It was like stepping into heaven. No less than perfect."

The Simple Gift is the compelling story of 16 year old Billy, who trades the soulless tyranny of his father's home and the tediousness of high school for a life of no fixed address.

This free verse novel, by one of Australia's most popular poets, is a life-affirming look at humanity, generosity and love.

ISBN 0 7022 3133 9

A Dangerous Girl

Catherine Bateson

Merri, John, Leigh and Nick are positioned like the four points of a gameboard. Gentle John is Dungeon Master and a craftsman of wood, but can he master the ambitious, volatile Leigh?

His sister Merri is seduced by the glamour of the stage, but her attention turns to Nick and his email haikus … Emotional games run high in this crossover of fantasy and reality.

ISBN 0 7022 3168 1

The Darkness

Anthony Eaton

In the small coastal town of Isolation Bay, a shadow hangs over the lives of Rohan Peters and his mother Eileen. Bound together by small-town superstition, their lives are dominated by fear.

Into this setting comes Rachel, a girl on the run from her own dark history. Together, their pasts come crashing down on them in an event that will change their lives forever.

ISBN 0 7022 3152 5

After January

Nick Earls

This January is different. School is over for Alex Delaney and the waiting for his tertiary offer is killing him.

He's not expecting much from January — bodysurfing, TV, but mainly waiting. So he's not ready for the girl who cuts past him on a wave, a girl who throws him right off balance …

ISBN 0 7022 2823 0

The Last Race

Celeste Walters

After years of dedicated training, Philippa has qualified for the Olympics but her best friend and rival lies in a coma in hospital.

Why is Philippa wracked with guilt? And why does she tell her mother that she cheated?

This gripping novel explores the lives of two gifted swimmers in their last year of high school. For them the stresses of study and approaching adulthood are compounded by a gruelling training regime.

ISBN 0 7022 3172 X

The View from Ararat

Brian Caswell

This powerful sequel to Deucalion takes place a century later. Deucalion's existence is threatened by a plague of immense proportions. Politicians, individuals, and the Elokoi are faced with a threat of such magnitude that social justice could be the first casualty and civilisation the second.

ISBN 0 7022 3067 7

Yumba Days

Herb Wharton

For young Aborigine, Herbie, his Yumba is a village peopled
with family and friends who keep an eye on him and his mates.
But there's always escape to the hop-bush plain or the saddle in
this whip-cracking adventure full of larrikin fun and ancestral
legends told under the stars.

ISBN 0 7022 3113 4

McKenzie's Boots

Michael Noonan

As a young soldier in New Guinea during World War Two, Rod
McKenzie is an unlikely hero — even his oversized boots are the
joke of the battalion.

   Hunting for butterflies one day, Rod encounters a Japanese
soldier with the same pastime, leading him to question wartime
notions of friend and enemy.

ISBN 0 7022 2070 1